THE
CRYPTID FILES

P.K. HAWKINS

SEVERED PRESS
HOBART TASMANIA

DARK ISLAND

Copyright © 2020 by Severed Press

WWW.SEVEREDPRESS.COM

ISBN: 978-1-922323-61-3

PROLOGUE

Jessica had looked forward to this weekend for a long time, so she was getting pretty annoyed that Brian was making it so miserable. With all the work she'd been putting into college, she didn't have a lot of time to herself, and what time she did have usually went into doing things that Brian wanted to do, things like bar crawls and keggers. Jessica wasn't at all interested in those sorts of things, but Brian was the first real boyfriend she'd ever had. She'd been too shy and introverted in high school to attract anyone's attention, so the fact that someone like Brian was with her now made her want to do anything at all to keep him by her side.

Now though, after a day out camping and hiking

in the wilderness, she wasn't sure how much she wanted to do with him anymore. He was a city guy to his core, but he'd seemed interested in going out into the forest and mountains with her. Soon after they'd started hiking though he'd gone straight into complaining about his feet. Now, on day two, it was obvious to her that he hadn't bothered to prep for the trip at all and had instead expected that all they'd be doing the entire time was getting naked with each other in a tent. Not that she would have complained about that, but they could do that anywhere. Out here there were other things to do, things she couldn't do most of the time, like fish and hike and just enjoy nature.

"Nature sucks," Brian mumbled from behind her on the trail. It was approximately the ninth time today he'd said it, or at least the ninth time Jessica had heard it. Honestly he might have said it a lot more when she couldn't hear, but her hearing it seemed to be the point. "Why can't you be into something less likely to get me blisters on my feet? Something like sewing."

"You constantly mock people who sew," Jessica said. "And the blisters wouldn't be there if you'd followed my advice and broken in your boots before the trip."

"I thought we were going to be knocking boots, not keeping them on," he muttered. Right there, in that moment, Jessica realized their relationship was going to end as soon as they got home. They were definitely not right for each other anymore, if they ever had been in the first place. Jessica knew that there was a spot up ahead on the trail where they could easily loop back around and start heading back early, and although it sucked that her time out here was going to be cut short, it was probably for the best. If she tried to keep this going for the whole weekend, it would only be more miserable for both of them.

"It looks like there's a spot up ahead where we can rest if you want," Jessica said. She thought about adding in what she was thinking, about turning around and ending the trip early, but she thought it would be better if they had a breather first, just in case she was tempted to just blurt out that she wanted to end other things as well. That would best wait until they weren't in the middle of nowhere.

Brian looked around at the clearing she pointed

out as though he expected a comfy chair to magically pop out of the ground, and when one didn't, he scowled at a fallen tree. "What, am I supposed to sit on that?"

"Or you can keep standing," Jessica said. "It's fine by me." She took a seat closer to the broken end of the tree and did her best to ignore him as he sat next to her and pulled off his boots. Idly inspecting the splintered portion of the tree, she realized the break was still fresh. The tree had been old and large enough that they could both sit on the trunk comfortably, so it wasn't something that should have been able to easily break unless it was diseased or dead, but the wood inside looked healthy.

"I can't wait to get back to somewhere civilized," Brian said. "Some place with beer."

"What do you think could have broken this tree like this?" Jessica asked.

"Don't know, don't care," Brian said. "It was probably blown over in a storm or something."

"I don't think so," Jessica said. "And it doesn't look like it was chopped down, either. It looks almost like something came along and pushed it over."

"Like what? A bear?" Brian asked, suddenly sounding alarmed.

"I don't know. Maybe," Jessica said. She doubted it, though. There certainly were bears in this area, but she didn't know of any bear that would be large and strong enough to knock over a tree like this, or even why a bear would do it in the first place. Still, when she looked closer at the bark, there did appear to be fibers on it that might have been bear fur. She picked up a strand of the fur and started to examine it, but before she could look at it too closely, Brian was standing up and stumbling away from the tree as quickly as he could go.

"If there's bears around here then I'm definitely not sticking around," Brian said.

"Brian, where the hell are you going?" Jessica asked. "You can't just go wandering off up here, especially without even putting your boots back on."

But he wasn't listening to her. With one boot left behind at the tree and the other still in his hand, he was already moving at a fast jog back the way they had come. Before Jessica could say anything more he disappeared into the bushes off the side of the path.

"Not that way!" Jessica called out after him. "You're going to break your neck running willy-nilly through the underbrush like that."

From somewhere deeper in the foliage, Brian made a surprised grunting sound, then went silent.

Jessica froze. Although she had no idea why, her every instinct suddenly told her she needed to be in fight-or-flight mode. "Brian?"

There was still no sound, not him complaining, not him blundering through the underbrush, not even him crying out as he stubbed his toe on something.

Go, she thought to herself. *Get back down the trail as fast as possible.* It was a stupid thought, she realized. That was what she would have screamed at someone to do if they were in a horror movie, but this was real life. And in real life, something didn't just come out of the woods to kill someone. In real life, someone as incompatible with nature as Brian was much more likely to stumble off a ledge and down the steep side of the mountain. And if that were the case, then if she ran he would be as good as dead by the time she got back with help.

"Brian? If you're playing a joke, it's not funny," Jessica said. "It can be dangerous out here if you goof around."

She thought she finally heard something from the direction he had disappeared in. It sounded like something running away through the brush, something very large. *Oh crap, it really is a bear*, she thought, *or maybe a mountain lion*. Whatever it was, it seemed to be moving away from her at a very fast pace. Again she fought the urge to run, reasoning that running would only make her look like prey to something like that, and whatever it was must not be in the immediate vicinity anymore anyway. And she couldn't leave Brian behind, especially if he might be hurt. She might be fully prepared to dump him as soon as they got back to town, but that sure as hell didn't mean she wanted him harmed in any way.

"Brian? If you can hear me, call out to me."

Cautiously, she followed the path he had taken into the underbrush, moving slowly and watching her footing carefully just in case there was indeed some kind of drop-off he hadn't seen. She didn't get far, though, before her foot squelched in something damp and squishy.

"What the fuck?" she whispered, raising her

boot to see what she'd stepped in. It came up dripping red.

"Oh shit. Brian? Brian, can you hear…" She stumbled a couple of steps forward into a patch where the brush was more cleared away. That was finally where she saw the source of the blood.

The two arms lying there with blood sprayed all around them had clearly belonged to Brian. She recognized the small tattoo on his left forearm. That was all there was here, though, to show that Brian, or at least part of him, had been here. Both arms looked like they had been ripped off his body right at the shoulder joints, and the gore, bone, and muscle hanging from them implied that, whatever had removed them, it hadn't been done with any kind of sharp blade. In fact, they looked more like they had been ripped straight off of his body.

Okay, she thought to herself with the sort of calm that could only come with sudden, inexplicable trauma. *Now I can run.*

Jessica turned and did exactly that. A few seconds later, something else in the forest, just as she had feared, started to give chase.

CHAPTER ONE

This wasn't exactly Agent Bradley Tennyson's first day on the job, but it was the first day he could rightfully, truly be called "agent," and he was certain that he was prepared for anything at all that the agency might throw at him. Or at least, that was what he had thought before he took a seat at the division head's desk and heard who his first ever partner was going to be.

"The Crag? You have got to be kidding me," Tennyson said.

His boss looked at him with a raised eyebrow. "I'm surprised you've already heard of Agent Crag."

"Everyone in the academy knows about the Crag," Tennyson said. "The teachers use him as a cautionary story about what happens when you spend too many years in the agency without a vacation. They say your brain breaks down and you become a basement-dwelling troll. Uh, but please don't tell him I said that."

"On the contrary," his boss said. "I'm willing to bet that George would take that description as a compliment. And he would definitely find it amusing that the academy thinks of him as a what-not-to-do story."

"Am I being punished?" Tennyson asked. "When I was doing my thing at the academy, did I fuck the kid of some higher up that wants to punish me now?"

"Not at all. Just the opposite." The division head looked at the monitor of his computer, where presumably he had Tennyson's file pulled up. "You were at absolutely the top of your class in most things. And you weren't shy about letting people know it, too. You were brash and you were a braggart. You could also back it up with actions. And I heard all about the Sandman incident right after it happened."

Tennyson couldn't help but give a cocky grin.

"That was pretty amazing, wasn't it?"

His boss ignored Tennyson's moment of patting himself on the back. "But that kind of attitude doesn't usually get people busting down the door to partner with you. There's plenty of concerns about how you'll actually be out in the field. Very few of the senior agents I approached about possibly partnering with you were too keen on the idea that you might completely go off and do your own thing when they needed you by their side the most. Few agents, that is, except for George."

Tennyson sat back in his chair and thought about everything he'd ever heard about Agent George Crag, or simply "the Crag" to most people. Although Tennyson had never actually seen the man, the word was that the Crag was several years past where he should have retired, yet he was still a solidly built, in-shape man. He had his office deep in the furthest bowels of the agency's main building. What exactly he did down there, no one was quite sure, but he had a reputation for pursuing the kinds of cases that most people ignored as the ravings of lunatics. "So you're saying he actually asked for me?" Tennyson asked.

"He did," the division head said. "He saw your files and said you reminded him of himself when he was young enough to still have something like idealism."

"I don't know if idealism is a word I would ever use for myself, sir."

"Well George did. And here's the thing about him: he's not down there in his little basement cave because he's been exiled down there or anything. He's there because he wants to be. He's saved the bacon of many a senior agent, and he had favors to call in."

"So he used them to become the proverbial monster in the dungeon instead of taking your job?" Tennyson asked incredulously.

"Not my job. My boss's job. Hell, maybe even his boss. He really could have gone that far up the agency. But that's not what he wanted. He wanted freedom to pursue his own work, and he got it. He wanted all the resources available to do that work, and he got it. So when he spoke to me and my superiors and said, 'I want Tennyson,' then guess what?"

"He got it," Tennyson muttered. "Don't I have

any say in this, though? I mean, what the hell would I even be doing with him? Not to sound too full of myself, but you've seen everything I can do. My aptitude tests, my shooting scores, those would all be wasted being his lackey in some moldering corner of the basement."

"A word of advice, Tennyson: if you ever have to say 'not to sound too full of myself,' then you are definitely way too full of yourself," the boss said. "You might want to tone it down a little bit if you ever do want to get a better assignment."

Tennyson frowned. "Yes sir."

"Because I do intend to give you a better assignment. Look, all you have to do is humor the old man for a bit. George goes through partners very quickly. He always finds something about them he doesn't like and gets one of us to assign him another one. In all likelihood, you'll only be with him for one case. You can handle a single case, right?"

"Absolutely I can."

"Good. So just be the old man's partner for a week or so, and when you're done, provided you've proven you're really as great as your instructors made you out to be, you'll probably end up with your pick of the best assignments out there." The division head stood up, a clear indication that this conversation was almost over. "Do you know how to get down to Agent Crag's lair?"

"Lair?" Tennyson asked. "You actually call it a lair?"

"You will, too, once you've seen it."

"I've heard roughly where it is. The sub-basement, back of the cold records room, right?"

"That's the place. You better get going. He told me that you were already going to have a busy first day."

Tennyson wasn't sure if he should be excited about that or not.

Finding his way to the Crag's office turned out to be a little more difficult than he had anticipated. It turned out that the deeper levels of the complex were maze-like and ill-kept, with dust over everything and lights flickering overhead as though they were able to fail and plunge Tennyson into some surrealistic labyrinth. He kept taking wrong turns at unclear signage, and after five minutes he started to get the sensation that maybe he'd fallen asleep in the division head's office and was having some kind of weird nightmare. Finally, though, he saw a light at the end of a dark hallway illuminating a large room full of file boxes on old metal shelves. Going into the room, however, didn't make any of this feel any less dreamlike.

Tennyson knew there were several cold case records rooms in the facility, but he doubted any of the other ones looked this cavernous and dilapidated. Some of the shelves full of moldering boxes went all the way up to the ceiling twenty feet above him. And the further he went down the rows of shelves, the older and more damaged the boxes seemed to be. Some of them even looked like they had the dark brown stain of long-dried blood on them, although that could have been a trick of the light.

And somewhere, far at the back of all of this, he could hear a scratchy old voice muttering and cursing quietly to itself.

"Agent Crag?" Tennyson called out. "Um, it's Agent Bradley Tennyson. I'm supposed to be your new partner."

"Ah yes, the fresh meat for the grinder is here," the voice called back. "Come on all the way to the back. Follow your nose, if you have to. The moldier it smells, probably the closer you are to me."

Tennyson thought at first that he was making a joke about his age, but the closer he got the more of a mildew smell there was in the air. It was the Crag that was causing it though. Agent Crag really had chosen to put his work space in the deepest, dankest, gloomiest spot of the sub-basement. The boxes here were so old that the cardboard was disintegrating or splitting apart from ancient water damage. There was a cleared-out space among the shelves where a number of rusting metal tables were heaped with books, boxes, and a number of murky jars that appeared to have some kind of pickled specimens inside, although the specimens were so old and mushy that nothing could actually be identified.

The Crag stood at one of the tables with a laptop open in front of him, the only modern thing Tennyson could see in the entire room, and even that was a model about ten years out of date. "Out of date model" could also be said of the Crag himself, although it was immediately obvious that out-of-date was nowhere near the same as being in bad shape. Despite his clearly advanced years and papery, liver-spotted skin, the Crag had the height of a pro wrestler, and almost a build to match. He was obviously a man who still spent long hours in the gym. His hair was pure white and neatly trimmed, and there was a mustache on his face that would have been all the rage in the eventies. Despite the decrepitude of everything around him, the Crag wore an immaculately clean and pressed black suit that demanded respect from anyone who saw it.

Tennyson had to admit it. He hadn't wanted to be, but he was impressed. That still didn't mean that he was happy to be wasting his time with this old fossil.

"No, young man," Crag said. "I am most definitely not an 'old fossil.'"

Tennyson blinked. "How did you... did you just..."

"No, I didn't read your mind. I knew that's what you were thinking because that's what *everyone* thinks of me. And they can go right ahead and keep doing so for all I care. It means they're not prepared for me when I come for them."

"If you don't mind me asking, how old are you?"

"I do mind, but I'll still tell you: I'm old enough

that I was at this agency when you were still a come-stain in your daddy's drawers."

"That's, uh, colorful."

"It's also an old, over-used joke that was never actually funny in the first place, and you should have called me on it." Crag stepped away from the computer and looked Tennyson up and down. "Everything I've heard says you're the best recruit to graduate from the academy in years."

Tennyson started to make a smart-ass comment, then thought better of it because the older agent seemed to be testing him. Then he thought better of it again, because he wasn't going to let this guy just push him around, no matter how long and storied his career at the agency might be. "Decades, actually. Probably the best since before I was a... you know."

The Crag smirked, and Tennyson felt like he'd been right. He'd been testing Tennyson in some way, all right, and he gave the impression that the younger agent had passed whatever it was. "Well then, let's prove it right away, shall we?" Crag turned back to the table and grabbed a thick manilla folder that had been sitting there on top of a pile of junk. "Let's go on to your first case."

"Wait, now?" Tennyson asked. "I just got here. Shouldn't I at least get myself settled in around here?"

"No sense in that if you can't handle the kinds of things that are going to be thrown at you when you work with me. I've already picked out something fresh that's right in my normal jurisdiction, and we're going to see how long you can last."

Suddenly Tennyson felt conflicted. He still didn't actually want to work with this man on whatever forgotten cold cases he'd decided were his forte. But this felt like a blatant challenge. He wanted out of here as fast as possible, yet he wanted to make sure this elder knew exactly how good of an agent he would be losing when Tennyson went on to bigger and better things.

"There's nothing you can throw at me that I won't be able to handle," Tennyson said.

"You say that now," Crag said as he led him over to a door in the wall. Beyond it was a staircase leading up into the more well-lit portions of the building. Damn it. If Tennyson had known about that, he could have avoided getting lost on the way here. "But we'll see what you say later. Because this thing I'm going to throw at you? It's big. So big, that's literally its first name."

He vanished up the stairs before Tennyson could ask him what he meant, and Tennyson followed.

CHAPTER TWO

Crag was quiet about their destination all throughout their flight, which ended up taking them to Washington. He even stayed infuriatingly silent as they got a rental car and drove for a couple of hours into the less inhabited regions of the state. He wouldn't even engage in any small talk, leading Tennyson to sleep for most of the ride. When Crag finally did start talking, it startled Tennyson, but he was happy to finally be getting on with whatever this case was.

"We're here," Crag said as the car approached a small town on a back road. "Welcome to the site of your first actual case as an agent."

"Here? Uh, this place doesn't even look like it's large enough to have a name," Tennyson said.

"It does, but only barely," Crag said. "I kid you not, welcome to the town of Shacksville."

"Shacksville," Tennyson muttered. "Seriously, I think I'm in hell."

And if ever there was a town that lived up to its name, it was this one. If Crag hadn't slowed down as they entered the town and instead continued driving at the speed they'd been going on the highway, they would have blown right through it in the space of a few breaths. None of the houses were particularly large or elaborate, and there only seemed to be a total of four buildings that weren't domiciles: a church, a small clinic, a diner, and a motel. Crag pulled into the parking lot of the motel, and as he started to get out, Tennyson finally couldn't take waiting anymore.

"Okay, so can you please tell me why we flew all the way out to the middle of nowhere, then drove ever further into nowhere, and are now looking like you want to stay in nowhere for at least a night?"

"Shacksville isn't completely nowhere," Crag pointed out. "You can find it on a map. People live here."

"But I'm pretty sure we're not even within the

agency's jurisdiction anymore."

"You'd be surprised how little jurisdiction matters in the cases I investigate," Crag said.

Tennyson wasn't completely sure what that meant, and he wasn't sure he wanted to, either. Crag was the senior agent here, and if he said they were within their jurisdiction, Tennyson was just going to go with it and plead plausible deniability if this came back to bite them in the ass later. "Just tell me already. Why are we here?"

"We're here to investigate at least one murder," Crag said. "Possibly two. And, if I'm correct, maybe find the culprit to a whole lot of other murders and missing persons from the past twenty or thirty years as well."

Finally Tennyson perked up. Not that he was excited about the idea of everyday people getting killed, but finally there was a hint that this case had something meaty to it, something he could sink his teeth into for his first ever true field work. "Okay, you've got my attention. Tell me more."

"Not yet," Crag said. "Let's check into our rooms first and then we can go over to that diner and discuss it over coffee. Food, too, if you've got the stomach to talk about blood and guts while you eat."

Tennyson bristled at the subtle implication that he might not have the fortitude for such things. "I could demolish a cheeseburger about now, sure, but then I want some answers."

They both checked in at the motel's main office, which looked like something out of the seventies but had a cheerful young woman behind the desk that Tennyson shamelessly flirted with before they went down the street to the diner. True to his earlier request, he ordered three cheeseburgers and an order of fries while Crag opted for just a slice of cherry pie and a cup of coffee.

"Damn, that's really fine," Crag said as he took a sip of his drink.

"Whatever," Tennyson said around a mouthful of meat and bread. "So get to it. What's going on in Shacksville that could possibly merit us being here? If it were just murder, it wouldn't be something the agency would involve itself in."

"The agency only has the barest idea that we're here," Crag said. "And they certainly don't know why."

"But didn't you have to report to the division

head before we left?"

"I've saved that asshole's butt more times than I can count, both in the field and in the bureaucratic shit pile that's constantly trying to drown him. He lets me do pretty much whatever I want on the condition that I don't ever talk about it. And that's going to have to go for you, too, Tennyson. You may see things you're not ready to see with me, and the only way you and I will continue to have the freedom to see them is if we don't make any noise. No press, and only the barest actual reports filed."

"Um, okay. Whatever. Quit being cryptic already and get to the action."

"Hold your horses. You'll get that soon enough." Tennyson paused to take a bite of his pie, intentionally taking as long as possible to enjoy it, or possibly just because he enjoyed pissing Tennyson off. Tennyson managed to keep from saying any smartass comments until Crag swallowed. Apparently confident now that he could make his young partner be patient when it was required, Crag finally started explaining.

"Yesterday morning the body of a young woman was found near here," he said. "A twenty-year old college student named Jessica LaCroix. Two days earlier she and her boyfriend, Brian Perez, came up to this area to do a little hiking and camping. That's the only thing Shacksville really has that comes close to an industry: there's a couple little used trails into the mountains not far from here, and this is usually people's last stop before they go there and first stop when they leave."

"Cause of death?" Tennyson asked, trying not to sound too excited at someone's unfortunate circumstances.

"Good question," Crag said. "There isn't really a good coroner around here, so the reports so far are inconclusive. I can show you the file when we get to the scene, and we'll see what you have to say about it. I'm telling you right now though that she definitely didn't fall and break her neck or any other kind of simple accident. Whatever happened to her, it was very violent."

Tennyson noticed he hadn't mentioned anything about finding Perez with her. "Was it the boyfriend?"

"Under normal circumstances, the boyfriend or the husband would usually be the best place to start looking in these kinds of cases," Crag said. "But you're going to learn pretty quickly that I don't pick cases that have anything to do with normal circumstances. I'll humor you for the moment, though, and say that no one has seen the boyfriend at all since her body was discovered. Other agents would probably start by putting a BOLO out for Perez."

"But not you?" Tennyson asked.

"I'm telling you this right now, kid, and you can choose to believe me or not, but we're not going to be finding the boyfriend. Not alive, at least."

"Why are you so sure of that?"

"Because as I told you before, this place around here has a history. LaCroix isn't the first hiker around here to meet a gruesome end. The fifty-mile radius around this town has a three hundred percent higher disappearance rate than any other comparable backwater in the country."

Tennyson quietly whistled. Suddenly this looked like it really *might* be exactly the kind of case he wanted to start with after all. His brain started making connections, and he looked around the diner with sudden paranoia. There was the waitress, the cook in the back, and a trucker-looking guy over in the corner reading a newspaper. None of them looked like they were trying to listen in on this conversation, but Tennyson dropped his voice lower just in case. "A serial killer? You think it might be one of the locals?"

Crag snorted, although Tennyson didn't have any clue what he might find so funny. "A local. Sure. I guess I would say that, after a fashion."

"I don't get the joke," Tennyson said.

"You will eventually." Crag polished off the rest of his pie and didn't bother to elaborate.

"So there's extra disappearances around Shacksville," Tennyson said. "But what about bodies? If someone were doing this for so long, why would they suddenly leave a body where it could be found? That would be an awfully big change in pattern."

"Yeah, it is," Crag said. He took out his wallet and put enough money down on the table under his plate to pay for both of their meals and still leave an extremely generous tip for the waitress. "That's what worries me, and that's why I wanted to get out here with a partner as soon as possible. I've been monitoring this area for a while, but something feels different about this one. I'm getting the feeling that if something isn't done soon, then simple disappearances aren't going to be the biggest problem anymore. And I don't want what happened to this college girl to start happening on a larger scale."

"So are you going to take me to where the body was found and show me the file, or not? Because if you're really that worried, then sitting around here isn't going to help any."

"That's where we're off to next," Crag said as he stood up. "You'll want to come back with me to the motel first, though."

"Why?" Tennyson asked.

Crag pointed at his shiny black polished shoes. "Because we're going to want to be wearing something a whole lot hardier than these where we're going."

CHAPTER THREE

To get to the actual scene of the crime, they had to go down several backroads that led a little deeper into the mountains around them. It wasn't terribly far, less than ten minutes by car, but most of the roads they took weren't well maintained, making for a bumpy ride, and the final one they stopped on was little more than gravel. Crag pulled over in a small area off to the side that was obviously intended for parking, but it was overgrown with weeds and no one else was here at the moment.

Tennyson got out of the car and looked around at their environment. Crag had said they probably wouldn't change their clothes completely just yet, as this was just to get a feel for the murder scene, but they might need something more rugged later. As such, Tennyson still wore his suit, but he'd shed his tie and changed into a pair of hiking boots. Crag had done the same, and he was making no effort to hide the gun he had strapped in under his jacket. He even made sure to loosen it from its holster as he joined Tennyson outside the car. Tennyson wasn't sure exactly what kind of trouble he thought they were going to get in way out here, but Tennyson followed Crag's lead and made sure his gun was ready to draw at a moment's notice.

"So how far is it to the murder site?" Tennyson asked.

"We're practically standing at it," Crag said. He grabbed a folder from inside the car before walking fifteen feet over the start of what looked like a little-used trail up the mountain. Although the spot had been cleaned, Tennyson saw right away that the dirt here was darker than all around it, probably from blood that had soaked into it.

Crag flipped open the folder to show the photos of the dead body that had been lying here only a day prior. Although Tennyson knew he was supposed to be looking at the photos, he temporarily found himself more entranced by the folder itself. "So, do you not know how to use a tablet or something?"

"I probably know how to use one better than you ever will," Crag said. "But if you stick around with me, you'll find that a lot of the files we'll be pulling from the archives have never been digitized. No one bothered with it. They thought they were too ridiculous to merit serious investigation in this day and age. It's just easier to add new things to these old folders than it is to go through all the records in my office and put them on a computer."

Tennyson looked at a few of the photos in the folder and blanched. He'd seen plenty of photos of dead bodies at the academy, along with a few actual cadavers, and he knew he would see plenty more before his hopefully long career as an agent was up. But this was his first real one during a case, and he couldn't help but remember that the dead woman in the pictures had been an actual, breathing person up until recently. "So give me a better idea of what I'm looking at here," Tennyson said.

"Mostly I would think the photos speak for themselves," Crag said. "You're looking at a young woman in her prime who was viciously beaten to death."

"It's, um, actually kind of difficult to figure out which pieces of gore and body parts belong where, though."

"According to the half-assed job that the local coroner seems to have done, the official cause of death seems to be that she was beaten to death," Crag said.

"That seems to support the idea to me that it was the boyfriend," Tennyson said.

"Maybe under other circumstances," Crag said. "Being beaten to death would imply a crime of passion, not something premeditated. Except take a closer look at these pictures. Does this really look like the kind of beating handed out by a boyfriend, psycho and enraged or not?"

Tennyson was quiet for several minutes as he looked through the pictures, forcing himself to really study them whether he wanted to or not. After some time, he began to make a little sense of the carnage and stated what he thought he was seeing. "Blunt force trauma in most cases. Definitely looks like she was hit, and judging from some of these marks I could believe it might have been a fist, although if it was the boyfriend, he would have to be one beefy individual to leave marks that big."

"Good eye to start with," Crag said. "What else?"

"The blunt force wasn't all of it, maybe not even most of it. If you look here, and here, I'd guess that her joints were dislocated." He flipped to the coroner's report, then nodded as he read it. "Not just dislocated, either. It's almost like… well, that can't be it. That wouldn't make a lot of sense."

"Maybe it does, maybe it doesn't," Crag said. "Tell me what you're thinking."

Tennyson looked over the photos again. The longer he stared at them, the more desensitized he became to the senseless carnage and the more his mind started treating it like a puzzle. "It almost looks like someone tried and failed to quarter her."

The Crag raised an eyebrow at him. "Quarter?"

"You know, like that old punishment that would be done with horses. A person would be tied by the ankles and wrists to four different horses facing away from the person. They would all go running off in different directions and tear the person limb from limb."

Crag nodded like it wasn't the craziest thing he'd ever heard, even though Tennyson himself didn't see how something like that could possibly be the case here. "I think you're actually going in the right direction with this."

"How the hell could I be going the right direction?" Tennyson asked. "This narrow little path isn't large enough for four horses, and judging from the blood spatters in the photos, it doesn't look like she was murdered somewhere else and then brought here. And why would anyone go to the effort to set something like that up out here?"

"You're taking what I just said too literally," the Crag said. "Obviously this wasn't an actual quartering, especially since you can see from the picture that her limbs are still on her body."

"Uh, mostly," Tennyson said, looking specifically at one particular photo showing the place where the woman's left leg should have connected at her hip. The skin was ripped and torn, and the visible bones underneath were not where they were supposed to be.

"So someone or something tried to pull her limbs off, but wasn't quite successful. As you said, the setup here isn't exactly ideal for horses, and that method of killing her would have probably been successful in dismembering her. So think, Tennyson. What else would have been capable of doing this kind of damage with a minimal amount of space or preparation?"

Tennyson felt like Crag was trying to lead him to a specific answer, but he had no idea what it could possibly be. Falling back on sarcasm, he shrugged his shoulders and said, "I don't know, a gorilla?"

The Crag actually smiled at him, and somehow that made Tennyson nervous. "I bet you think that was a smartass answer that couldn't possibly be anywhere close to the truth, don't you?"

"Wait, what?" Tennyson asked. "Please tell me you're not actually suggesting that Jessica LaCroix was killed by a rampaging gorilla."

"No, of course not."

"Okay, good."

"This is the Pacific Northwest. There're no gorillas here. How would it even get here? That's a completely nonsensical answer that defies logic."

"I know, I was just…"

"She was killed by Bigfoot," Crag said.

"…trying to… Wait. What?"

"Or Sasquatch, if you prefer. Actually, I should say *a* Bigfoot or *a* Sasquatch. Otherwise I'm implying that there's only one of them in the world, and obviously I'm not. That would be silly."

For the briefest of moments, Tennyson thought the Crag was making his own peculiar attempt at humor. But when he stared at Tennyson with a dead serious face, one of his eyebrows cocked as if challenging Tennyson to not believe his ridiculous assertion, the younger agent realized his new partner was really making this suggestion.

"Bigfoot," Tennyson said incredulously. "That's what this is all about? That's why you took this case and flew us all the way to the ass-end of the country to a tiny little shithole town? You wanted to investigate a case that some idiot thinks might be Bigfoot."

"To be clear, the only 'idiot' suggesting it's Bigfoot is me," Crag said. "So you may want to watch what you say to your elders, you little asshole. No one else is saying. None of the people in town are suggesting it, and I bet when we bring it up with them, they'll deny it. But I know that's exactly what this is."

"Do any of your superiors know this is what you're investigating?" Tennyson asked. He almost added "Do they know this is what you're wasting the time of one of their most brilliant young agents with?" but thought better of it. It might come across as him being cocky and overconfident about himself, even though it was completely true.

"Of course they do. They know all about the kinds of cases I prefer. And I know about enough skeletons in closets that let me do it with minimum interference."

Tennyson looked down at the spot where Jessica LaCroix had died along the trail. She absolutely deserved justice for what had been done to her, but there was no way she was going to get it with the Crag investigating things that didn't even exist instead of going after the real leads. Maybe Tennyson would still be able to pursue the boyfriend angle while the Crag went off and did his own crazy-pants thing.

"It's starting to get dark," Crag said. "We should get back to the town and call it a night. I'm betting we don't want to be out here after the sun goes down."

"Yeah, sure," Tennyson muttered. "Wouldn't want to get attacked by the missing link."

"The idea of a missing link is a scientific falsehood," Crag said as he walked back to the driver's side of the car. "It's more likely that Bigfoot is some kind of branch on the evolutionary tree that started to evolve away from a common humanoid ancestor long ago."

"Um, right, sure," Tennyson said as he got back in the car. "Definitely wouldn't want to investigate fucking Bigfoot in anything other than a scientific manner."

CHAPTER FOUR

Once they were both back at the motel and settled in for the night in their own separate rooms, Tennyson took some time to consider his options. After going back and forth about it in his mind many times, he finally decided to pull out his phone and call his department head.

He wasn't entirely certain what he intended to say, but he definitely wasn't expecting the boss to answer the phone the way he did.

"Ah, Tennyson. I figured I was about to get a call from you any minute now."

"Sir, I need to speak to you about… wait, what? Why would you be expecting me to call?"

"Because only seconds ago I just got done

speaking with Crag."

Tennyson's mouth worked for several seconds and he tried to figure out what to say, then finally answered. "Sir, do you have any idea what the hell he thinks we're investigating here?"

"Of course I do. He claims you're after a killer Bigfoot."

"And you believe him, sir?"

"Of course not. What do you think I am, deranged?"

"Then… then why are you letting him go on like this? Shouldn't you be ordering us to come back and stop wasting agency resources on things that don't exist?"

"If you know what's good for you, Tennyson, you'll think twice before you ever ask me that question again."

Tennyson thought back to what the Crag had said earlier about knowing of skeletons in closets and mouthed a curse. Whatever deep dark secret Crag knew about the department head, it was enough to convince their boss that he should be allowed to go on whatever wild goose chase he wanted.

There was a different approach Tennyson could

take though, so he switched the direction of the conversation. "You said before I went to meet him that he would likely want to get rid of me after not too long, right?"

He paused before answering. "I did say that, yes."

"Well, then you might as well pull me from the assignment now so we're not wasting any more of my time or the Crag's. I didn't agree with his ridiculous theory, so he's got to be just about ready to get rid of me, right?"

To Tennyson's surprise, the boss chuckled. "Oh my. This really is rich."

"What's rich?" Tennyson asked. "Wasn't that the reason Crag was on the phone with you? To complain about me?"

"On the contrary, our conversation was about exactly the opposite. He was telling me how very impressed he is with you. More impressed with any potential partner he's ever worked with."

Tennyson used his free hand to rub the bridge over his nose. He honestly thought he was getting a headache over this situation. "Please tell me you're joking."

"No joke at all. Crag says you're perfect, and assuming you survive your first case, he wants to keep you on with him permanently."

"Survive? What? What the flying fuck do you mean, survive?"

"Oh. Right. I guess I forgot to tell you. About half of Crag's potential partners don't stick around because they're dead."

"And… and that part really is a joke this time, right? Right?"

The boss hesitated for an awfully long time before laughing. "Yes, of course it's a joke that time."

Tennyson wanted to feel better, but he could not help but feel like that laugh had felt a little forced. "Um, okay. Good."

"It's more like a third of them."

"Sir, I, um…"

"Well, Tennyson, I'm sure you're going to have a very busy day with your new bestie tomorrow, so I'll let you go and get some sleep," the division head said. "I'm sure you're going to sleep very well tonight."

"Sir, wait. I'm…"

"Have a good night, Tennyson."

The boss hung up, leaving Tennyson to stare blankly at his phone and consider just where exactly he had gone wrong with his life.

He was about to put it away and get undressed for the night when the phone rang again. He thought for a moment that it would be the department head, calling him back to let him know that *all of this* was actually a joke, that the fun was over and he could come back to the agency now to get his real first assignment. Instead the words "The Crag" appeared on the screen, and Tennyson sighed before answering it.

"Yeah?" Tennyson asked.

"So did he hit you with the 'only a third of his partners died' bit or not? Because I wasn't sure if he would actually do it."

Tennyson shook his head in disgust. "So it really isn't true?"

"Of course it's not true. What kind of reputation do you think I would have if a third of my partners died in the middle of cases? I wouldn't be allowed to work in the field no matter how much dirt I knew about people. It's actually only a fourth of my partners."

"I'm hanging up now, Crag."

"Oh relax, kid. It's all just a little good-natured hazing for the new guy. But whatever he told you I said about you, it's the absolute truth. I really think I've found my perfect partner in you."

"You know, why are we having this discussion over the phone?" Tennyson asked. "Our rooms are just next door to each other. If you want to give me a pep talk and/or try to convince me that you're really not crazy, I can just come on over." Tennyson opened the door to his room and started in the direction of Crag's room, but before he could get more than a few feet he thought he heard something strange echoing out in the night air. In a middle-of-nowhere town like this, Tennyson normally would not have thought much of it. It could have been any number of animals making weird night noises out in the forests that surrounded the place. But upon hearing it, Tennyson's mind went back to the pictures of the murdered girl and, despite his best efforts, to the crazy claims of his partner.

"Tennyson? What is it?" Crag asked. "Something spook you?"

"I don't know. Maybe." The noise had sounded like a growl, or maybe a roar. Tennyson had lived for most of his life in cities, so he wasn't the best person to try to differentiate between the calls of various nocturnal creatures. But it sure hadn't sounded like anything he would imagine belonging out here.

"Give me a second to get my gun back on," Crag said. "I'll be right out there to join you."

"You don't have to do that. I'm sure it's nothing." And yet Tennyson found himself switching his phone to his off hand while using his main one to reach for his gun. He just had a weird, paranoid feeling that he might need it at any moment.

Slowly he walked past Crag's room and near the main office. Even though that probably was not the best thing for a motel to do when it was eighty percent vacant, the office seemed to be closed and the light was off. At the edge of the building he thought he could hear something like a growl again, but it was not echoing like before. This was definitely somewhere relatively close, like just down the main street.

Tennyson held his gun at the ready and then slowly peeked around the corner. Across the road and about two houses down he could see a hulking shape in the darkness, but from here he had no way of making out any details. He slowly brought his cell phone up to his ear and whispered into it. "Crag, are you still there?"

"I'm still here, kid. Tell me what it is you're seeing."

"There's a… a thing out here."

"No shit. Can you describe it for me, or are you just going to expect me to come up with a mental image by myself?"

From this distance and in this light, Tennyson was not entirely certain that he could. The only thing he could say for certain was that the proportions did not seem at all human. It was bipedal and had a head and arms, but that was about where the similarities ceased. The arms were unusually long, and the thing was tall, about seven feet if Tennyson was judging its height right next to the nearby buildings. But as the naked thing stepped out into the street, he could finally see that the most noticeable, out-of-proportion part of its body was its…

"…feet," Tennyson muttered into the phone disbelievingly.

"What was that, Tennyson? I don't think I heard you," Crag said. Despite the tenseness of the moment, however, Tennyson was certain that the older agent sounded nearly jovial.

"You know exactly what I just said, and you know exactly what I'm seeing!" Tennyson hissed into the phone. There was a light on in the window of the house closest to the creature, and Tennyson could see a brief glimpse of someone inside peering around a curtain. He could not get any details about them, though, because as soon as they saw the hulking creature stalking out into the street, they pulled the curtains closed and the light in the window shut off.

"Crag, if you would really like to say I told you so, then this is the best time," he hissed into his phone. "Get your old wrinkly ass out here now!"

"Even at my age, my ass muscles are still tighter than yours, kid," Crag's voice quietly said from behind him. Tennyson turned off his phone and then gestured for the older agent to look around the corner with him. "Take a peek if you want your idiotic theory proven true."

"Aren't you going to try to deny what you're seeing, saying it's a trick of the light or some guy trying to fake it in a giant hairy suit?"

The creature made a loud growl in the middle of the street. "Yeah, Crag, something tells me that's the real deal. I may be rational, but I'm not going to deny what I'm seeing and hearing with my own eyes and ears."

Both of them stayed crouched near the edge of the hotel as the creature – the Bigfoot, Tennyson now had to admit – lumbered out into the empty street of the town. For all the noise the thing had been making, no one other than them seemed inclined to be outside to investigate it. It stumbled around like it was drunk or confused, which would have been comical if it wasn't so large and draped in shadows. Tennyson looked at the gun in his hand and wondered how much good it would even do against something like that, although he didn't at all doubt his ability to hit it. No, he doubted that anything short of a shotgun or machine gun could take it down.

At this exact moment, at least, it didn't look like

they would need to try taking it out, as it wasn't doing anything more than stomping down the middle of the asphalt. If, however, it really was what had killed the girl, Tennyson sure didn't want it getting anywhere near anyone right now.

"Okay, so you've found your Bigfoot," Tennyson whispered to Crag. "What's the plan?"

"Plan? What plan? Why do you think I would have a plan?" Crag asked.

"You acted before like you knew there was going to be a Sasquatch here," Tennyson said.

"Sure, but that doesn't mean I've figured out how to trap or kill one," Crag said. "To be honest, I was thinking that I'd have at least another day to think about it before we finally came face to face with the thing."

Tennyson was about to say something snarky to him when someone shouted some distance down the street. "Hey! Hey you! You're not supposed to be here! Get out of here! Git!"

At first Tennyson thought the woman's voice might have been directed at him and Crag, but it was the Bigfoot that reacted by turning to the source of the voice and snarling. A woman with long bushy hair was standing outside of the clinic, and although Tennyson couldn't see much more of her than her outline, there was no doubt that she was holding a shotgun at the ready.

If he'd had the time, Tennyson might have yelled at her to get inside and let the professionals handle this, but before he could say any such thing the woman fired the shotgun into the air. The monster roared at her, but the noise did what it was supposed to do and sent it loping back in the direction it had come from. Tennyson ran down the street to see if he could see exactly where it went, but by the time he was between the houses where the Bigfoot had originally come from, there was no more sign of it.

Although he kept his gun out just in case, Tennyson lowered it and turned to glower at the woman. "Lady, whoever you are, I don't think you have any idea what you're interfering with."

"You're government agents investigating the fact that our Bigfoot just murdered some college girl, I'm betting."

Tennyson's jaw went slack with surprise. "Uh, yeah? How did you…"

Crag finally caught up beside him. "I'm betting that this woman here has seen a number of our kind wander through here investigating a few things, haven't you ma'am?"

"You're certainly the most official looking," the woman said. "I guess I'm going to have to go through the spiel where I explain the deep dark secret of Shacksville to a couple more government yahoos, ain't I?"

Tennyson was thrown off. He'd expected their first witness to interrogate in this case to be a little more intimidated by them, but this woman had just stared down a Bigfoot and acted like it was no big deal. The Crag, however, took it all in his stride. "If you'd be so kind, ma'am, we'd greatly appreciate it."

"You'd better come inside then," the woman said as she started walking to the front door of the clinic. "Any time I talk about this, people tend to need whiskey, and I've got plenty in a drawer in my desk.

Crag followed her inside like this was the most logical direction for their evening to take. Tennyson paused long enough to look back in the direction of the vanished Bigfoot, then cursed his life and followed them both.

CHAPTER FIVE

The interior of the clinic was about as rustic as such a place could be. The entire place was decorated in wood paneling with deer antlers hung high on the walls, making it seem at first more like some kind of hunting lodge than where a doctor might practice.

And this woman didn't strike Tennyson at all like his idea of a doctor, but from a couple of pictures on the walls along with framed degrees, he could only assume that's exactly what she was.

There was a receptionist's desk in the front room along with a cramped waiting area, but the desk had dust on it and pretty much nothing else.

Beyond that there were two rooms, one that might have been an examination room and the other that seemed to be this woman's office. She led them back to this office and gestured for the two of them to sit in the chairs in front of her enormous oak desk. Both of them declined and stayed standing. There was another door in here that looked like it went into a bathroom, and in one corner of the room there was a cot. Considering there were some clothes on hangers nearby it, Tennyson could only conclude that this wasn't just where she worked, but where she lived as well.

"I'm thinking that after what you two have just seen, you're probably going to need a drink," she said. She opened a drawer in her desk and pulled out a half full bottle of whiskey, then from another drawer pulled out two glasses and began pouring.

"None for me," Crag said. Tennyson, however, felt like he could definitely use some right about now. He accepted a glass from the woman and expected her to pour some for herself, but she put the second glass away and instead started drinking right from the bottle. In fact, from the faint odor about her, she had probably started before now.

"You going to tell us who exactly you are?" Tennyson asked after his first drink. He knew it was highly unprofessional to drink on the job, but "professional" people didn't exactly have run-ins with fucking Bigfoot, of all things, so apparently tonight was a night of exceptions.

"Why should I have to?" the woman said. "I belong here. You two very obviously do not. So the way I see, you guys are the ones who should be answering that question for me."

"If we told you we were from a government organization, would you believe us?" Crag asked.

"That little scrawny one there? Probably not. But you? Yeah, I'd believe it," the woman said. "You've got a certain way of carrying yourself. But walking a certain way isn't exactly a government issued ID, is it? Either of you have some kind of identification to back up what you say you are?"

"Not on us at the moment, no," Crag said. "We were both about to call it a night when that thing came out."

"Well, since I'm not actually surprised that the college girl's murder has drawn a little attention, I'll just go ahead and believe you both for now," she said. "But I still haven't caught any names from either of you."

"I'm Agent Tennyson," Tennyson said. "And this surly old fossil is Agent Crag."

"Or just *the* Crag to my friends," Crag said. "Or my enemies too, I suppose."

"Wish I could say I'm pleased to meet you both, but I'm not really. I'm Dr. Rebecca Aarons. The people of Shacksville either call me Doc Aarons or just Doc."

"You're an actual practicing doctor?" Tennyson asked, looking around the office. "No offense, but this isn't exactly the kind of doctor's office I'd want to go to for a checkup."

"Can't blame you for that," Doc said. "Pretty much everyone else in town would agree with you. But I'm the only person with a medical degree for at least twenty or thirty miles in any given direction, so if the locals get something that doesn't require surgery, then their best bet is to grit their teeth and come to me."

"As much as I'd like to discuss the minutia of small village life, we should probably cut to the chase," Crag said. "You don't seem too surprised by the fact that you just ran off a rampaging Bigfoot."

"And interestingly, neither do you," she responded. "Although your partner here doesn't seem as non-plussed as you are."

"He's new," Crag said. "Give him some time and he'll get used to it."

Tennyson wasn't sure he liked the sound of that, but he didn't have time to dwell on it now. "I'm assuming you've known about this Bigfoot for a while now."

"Of course I have. The whole town knows, more or less. Do you think that what happened to that college girl has never happened before around here?"

Tennyson glared daggers at the doctor. "You mean to tell us that murders like this have happened and you people just, what, never bothered to tell anyone?"

"Of course we've told people," Doc Aarons said. "What, you think we just don't bother reporting murders? We report every single one, and each one gets dismissed by people like you as just some wild animal or an accident. Shacksville has lived with the knowledge that there is a killer Bigfoot in the mountains around it for decades."

"But there's got to be people that investigate this sort of thing," Tennyson said. "Even amateurs. If there's really something out there, someone would have found proof by now."

"No, they wouldn't," Crag said. "A lot of the tourist traps out there known for cryptids are really nothing more than roadside attractions, and all the amateur Bigfoot hunters that flock to them are hacks of the worst kind. They couldn't find shit if it were sitting directly in their underwear. The real cryptid hotspots, people instinctually know better than to go anywhere near them."

"Except apparently for the people of Shacksville," Tennyson said.

"What, you think the town is small by accident?" Aarons asked. "There's a reason it's never grown bigger than this. The kind of people that still end up here are the ones so desperate to get away from the rest of the world that they'll ignore the strange goings-on in the mountains."

"Does everyone in town know about this thing?" Tennyson asked. He couldn't help but remember the moment earlier where someone had looked like they were looking out their window at the creature only to suddenly hide.

"No one talks about it," she said. "But yeah, I would say everyone knows. At the very least, everyone knows to keep their trap shut about it if they don't want the rest of the world to think they're crazy mountain hicks."

"And apparently they also know to keep inside when they hear a crazy woman screaming outside with a shotgun," Tennyson added.

"No, just this particular crazy woman," she said. She stopped talking long enough to take a swig from her whiskey bottle. "You could say that I have a bit of a reputation around here."

"I'm starting to see that," Tennyson said.

"You say you've reported this kind of stuff before," Crag said. "I find that interesting. You could say I pay attention to this sort of thing, but I haven't seen a lot of official reports. Mostly just rumors and speculation."

"That's probably because anything that happens around here isn't usually as violent as what happened to that girl. And probably her boyfriend, too. Most of the time it's disappearances or strange deaths. I don't know why, but this time seemed different. It's got a few people around here spooked. That's why I was ready to help you tonight. I figured I'd just kind of keep an eye out, and lo and behold, there it was and there you were."

"So if you know so much about this particular Bigfoot, do you have any idea of where we would start looking if we wanted to find where it's coming from?" Tennyson asked.

"If I could answer that, then someone around here would have gone after it already to shoot it and hang its head over their fireplace," Aarons said. "Possibly me."

"You don't have a fireplace in here," Tennyson noted.

The doctor winked at him and held up her whisky bottle before taking another drink. "Maybe not, but I've got plenty of booze, and anywhere there's enough alcohol, you can make a fire."

"There's a disturbing thought," Tennyson muttered.

"What about any idea of where we could start searching for more information?" Crag asked her.

"Well I sure wouldn't want to investigate it, but

if you're so dead set on this, then I'd start by going further along the trail where the girl's body was found," Doc Aarons said. "A larger than normal portion of the disappearances around here happen around that trail than anywhere else, and if you ask my opinion based on the way they found that girl's remains, she was running from something that came from further down it. If you want clues, that's your best start, but if you're expecting to somehow find the boyfriend's body, I wouldn't bet on it. People have searched that trail before when visitors went missing, and no bodies have ever been found along it."

"Until this girl, you mean," Tennyson added.

Doc Aarons seemed disturbed by that. "Yeah. Until this girl came along and threw off the pattern."

"It's getting late and I think we're going to need an early start tomorrow," Crag said to her, "but if we need to talk to you for more information, can we come back here and pick your brain?"

"Go ahead and pick it all you want, it's already pretty pickled!" she said, her words starting to slur slightly. Tennyson had his doubts that she would prove to be a very good source of information, but so far she had been better than nothing. He finished off what little was left in his glass and handed it to her, then they said their goodbyes and walked back to the motel.

At the doors to their rooms, Tennyson started to speak to Crag, but the older agent held up his hand. "Whatever you've got to say, it would be better to say it in the morning. I think we're going to have a long day ahead of us, and if I'm guessing right, you're going to have some trouble sleeping tonight anyway."

"Um, yeah," Tennyson said. "Maybe that's for the best."

"Then I'll see you in the morning," Crag said unceremoniously as he went through his door and closed it, leaving Tennyson alone to contemplate just how unbelievably fucked up this night had been.

CHAPTER SIX

Tennyson stayed very quiet when they met up bright and early the next morning outside of Crag's room. The two of them went to breakfast at the diner, but while Crag would occasionally talk about casual or inane things, Tennyson himself said absolutely nothing except to give his order to the waitress. Crag didn't bring up anything at all that had happened the night before, and he didn't even mention anything about the case. He seemed to be waiting for Tennyson to do the talking about it, but the younger agent had no idea where to even start, so he left it all unsaid for as long as he possibly could.

True to the Crag's prediction, Tennyson had slept extremely poorly the previous night. He'd woken up multiple times absolutely convinced that some giant hairy creature was in the room with him only to find himself completely alone in the quiet. And while he hadn't remembered his dreams when he'd woken up, he was pretty sure they were full of hulking shadows and screaming drunks with shotguns.

He did notice the waitress and a few of the locals giving both of them suspicious looks this morning, though, as the two of them ate their breakfast. Yesterday when they'd eaten here, no one seemed to have cared. But whether word had gotten around about the display in the street last night or not, there was very much a feeling that the two outsiders had riled something up and would be nothing but trouble. The waitress was cordial but cool with them, and when the time came for the two of them to settle their bill, she asked nonchalantly how long they were staying in town. When Crag said he wasn't sure, the look the waitress gave them clearly said they wouldn't be welcome to stay for long.

Finally, on the car ride back up to the beginning of the trail, Tennyson forced himself to say what he knew would have to come out of his mouth eventually. "I'm sorry."

The glance Crag gave him said that he knew exactly what Tennyson was talking about, but that he wasn't going to let it go so easily. "About what?"

"About doubting you," Tennyson said. "About not believing you. You were right. I can't believe I actually have to say this out loud, but you were right that the murder had been committed by a fucking Bigfoot, of all things."

"I'm going to accept your apology for now, Tennyson, but you better learn something really fast. I've been in this job for a very long time and have seen a shit-ton more than you have. It's one thing for you to doubt me for the first time, but that is never, ever going to be tolerated from you again, do you hear? You're not here with me to be the skeptic to my believer. You're here to be the backup I bring with me when I face strange things so I don't die. I say I think Bigfoot is a murderer, from now on I'm going to expect you to take my experience and believe it, do you understand me?"

Tennyson couldn't look him in the eye. "Absolutely, sir."

"Don't call me sir. I'm not your superior. I'm your partner. Your equal. But I'm also the one who has seen a lot more shit than you, and I'm going to expect you to remember that."

It was barely past eight in the morning when they pulled back into the space that worked as a parking lot for the trail into the mountains. Although it didn't look any different than it had the day before, Tennyson couldn't help but look at it all now in a new light. Seeing the spot where the body of Jessica LaCroix had been found, he could no longer picture the idea that the boyfriend could have been physically capable of the bloodbath. Not that he couldn't have killed the girl, but he now couldn't imagine how he had previously thought a normal human would have the ability to do what he had seen in those photos. He also now one hundred percent agreed with the Crag that the boyfriend had to be dead somewhere. The question now was where on earth could the body have gone.

"So what's the plan from here?" Tennyson asked Crag.

"Based on the way the girl was found, she was obviously running from our furry friend," Crag said.

"The logical thing to do would be to do our best at tracing her path back to where she would have started. That's where we're likely to find more clues, and if we're lucky we'll find the creature itself."

"I don't know if I'd say that was the luckiest possibility," Tennyson said. "After last night, I hope you don't mind if I keep my gun out the entire time."

Crag pulled his own weapon out of its holster. "I'd be disappointed in you if you didn't, kid."

They didn't move particularly fast along the trail up the mountain. Both of them stopped frequently to check along the sides of the trail for any clue that something other than human had been along here recently, but given that the murder had been several days back by now, Tennyson doubted they would find anything that was particularly fresh. There was no small-talk between them as they went, just total concentration on their job. After two hours up the mountain trail they still hadn't found anything of note, but Tennyson was anything but bored. If anything, he felt far more energized by this case now than he'd possibly thought he could be.

There was a small clearing on a plateau that looked like the kind of spot where hikers might take some time to rest, and it was there that they finally started to find things that might be useful. While Crag investigated the line of trees around the clearing, something caught Tennyson's eye and drew him for a closer look. After getting a really good view, he was truly convinced that he'd found their first real clue.

"Hey Crag, come take a look over here," Tennyson shouted. Crag turned to see him stooping next to a fallen tree and poking something with the edge of his shoe. When Crag got closer, he saw that the object was actually another shoe, or more specifically, a boot. It was untied and loosened, so whoever had left it here had taken it off on purpose, even if such a thing was probably very stupid all the way up here.

"That's an odd thing to find all by itself, don't you think?" Tennyson said.

"Odd, sure, but not as odd as that tree right next to it," Crag said.

"It's a tree. In a forest in the mountains," Tennyson said. "What's so odd about that?"

"A tree that's been knocked over. And before you act like a smartass and say that's not so odd either, just take a closer look at it."

Tennyson did, and he came to the conclusion pretty quickly that this tree hadn't been knocked over by any normal natural event. It also clearly hadn't been chopped down, judging from the incredibly rough break in the wood. Looking farther up the trunk of the tree, he could see a spot on the bark where something strong had clearly pressed against it and cracked large chunks off the bark.

"What are you thinking that means?" Tennyson asked.

"I'm thinking we're dealing with a creature big enough and strong enough that it can shove over a full-grown tree with its bare hands."

"At this time yesterday, I would have said you were full of it," Tennyson said. "But after last night? I might actually think you're right."

"And look here," Crag said, pulling a pen from a pocket in his jacket and using it to poke at the crushed area of the bark. He pulled it away with several coarse brown hairs on its tip. "What do you want to bet that if we got this DNA tested it would definitely not come back as any identifiable forest creature?"

"At this point, I am most definitely not taking that bet," Tennyson said. "So with the boot and the tree, this has to mean we're close to something, right?"

"Maybe," Crag said. "We should look around this whole area a little closer. There's got to be other clues that will lead us in the direction of this thing."

"You know, there's something we really need to discuss that we haven't yet," Tennyson said. "Let's say we do find this Bigfoot, and I still can't believe I'm actually saying that out loud, but what do we even do once we find it?"

"Well, we certainly don't let a rampaging monster that has killed at least one person and probably a whole lot more just continue to roam around."

"But are we going for the kill here, or are we going to try capturing it? How would we even try to capture a Bigfoot?"

"If it were to come down to us finding something we decided we should capture rather than kill, then I have connections for that sort of thing. Trust me, this isn't my first rodeo, and I'd know who to call to get dangerous things locked away for a long time. And if we were running up against some cryptid that wasn't really a danger after all, we'd let it go. But in this case? Based on what we've seen so far, I'm expecting we'll have to shoot to kill."

"So it's not just Bigfoot, then?" Tennyson asked. "There's other creatures like this that you've run into before?"

"This is what I've dedicated my life to investigating, kid."

"But why?"

"It's not like I've got some tragic backstory. The Loch Ness Monster didn't kill my mother or something. It's just that if I don't, no one else will."

"But doesn't it bother you that no one else seems to believe in it? Especially people at the agency?"

"It did before I got the funding and support I wanted. But now that I have a few things on a couple of influential people, it's a lot easier to do what I want to do and investigate whatever I want to investigate."

There wasn't a lot else worth noting in the clearing itself other than the tree and the boot. Where there was one boot, though, Tennyson knew there had to be another, and possibly still with a foot inside it. Crag, however, was the one who found their next clue. Just beyond the clearing's tree line he found a scrap of fabric that looked like it might have originally come from a t-shirt, and on it was a copious amount of brown stains that could only be human blood.

"This has to be the right direction to look," Crag said. He poked around in the underbrush, walking out of Tennyson's view before the younger agent could tell him to wait up. While he did that, Tennyson went over to an interesting looking rock formation that looked almost like someone or something might have shaped it by hand. "If we just…"

Crag's words cut off.

Tennyson turned in the direction where he had last seen the old agent, but he was seemingly gone.

CHAPTER SEVEN

Crag knew he was lying prone on top of a pile of bones even before he looked down to see what had broken his fall. He wouldn't say that being on top of bones was a common thing for him, but in his entire long career it had actually happened enough that he knew what the sensation felt like. The only question was what the bones had previously belonged to. He sat up, careful not to let any of the jagged pieces jab into him, and looked down to get a closer look at them. Many of them were smaller and had snapped under his weight, but some appeared to belong to much larger creatures. One ribcage nearby might have once belonged to a moose or possibly a horse of some kind. A skull some distance away had probably originally started out its life as a bear.

A few of them, however, looked very much like they had once belonged to humans, including several not too far away that still seemed to have some pieces of grisly meat clinging to them. Given what he knew, Crag would have been willing to bet his entire retirement plan that, if tested for DNA, these bones would prove to belong to the missing boyfriend of one Jessica LaCroix.

"Crag!" Tennyson's voice called from somewhere above. "Can you hear me? Are you alright?"

Crag looked up in the direction of his new partner's voice. The hole he'd fallen through was about nine or ten feet up with an irregular shape. Tennyson's head popped into view along with his hands on his gun like he thought he could possibly shoot the hole.

"I'm fine, kid, but judging from my surroundings I'm not exactly in any place I'd like to stay for an extended period of time," Crag said. He let Tennyson take a moment to process the large number of bones around him and paid very close attention to the way the rookie agent reacted. To Crag's satisfaction, he took the large number of bones in his stride rather than immediately freaking out. So far it did seem like the younger agent's reputation at the academy had been well-earned.

"What exactly happened?" Tennyson called down to him.

"The ground just seemed to give out under me," Crag responded. "Everything looked fine and stable, no sign of any kind of hole, and then all of a sudden I was down here."

"Give me a second to find some way to safely get down there with you," Tennyson said.

"No, don't do that," Crag called back. "Stay up there and keep watch. I'll investigate more down here. But if you can find some way to get me back up, that would be greatly appreciated."

As Tennyson disappeared from view, Crag started to crawl down off of the pile of bones he had landed on. The general shape of the room was a rough cylinder, but off to one side an archway went deeper into darkness. Crag took a look at that doorway for a long moment before deciding that he definitely was not set or ready to investigate down that direction further. It was a very large entrance, at least, suggesting that it could indeed lead to the creature they were seeking.

Instead of doing the dumb thing and going into the darkness alone and unprepared, he took a much closer look at the chamber around him and tried to make sense of it all. This was definitely where something was throwing the inedible remains of its meals, and unless there was a second non-Bigfoot cryptid that just so happened to be in the same territory as the creature they had seen last night, then logic dictated that the monster that had been roaming the streets of Shacksville was the same one responsible for this grisly pile. Already pretty sure what he would find, Crag took a closer look at the human-appearing bones he'd seen a minute earlier. There was no doubt whatsoever that they were fresh, still with rotting and stinking pieces of meat clinging to them, and Crag now had no doubt whatsoever that he'd finally located Jessica LaCroix's mysteriously missing boyfriend. Using his foot to rummage through the bones a little further, Crag found a few more that he was pretty sure had belonged to humans, including a few that disturbingly looked like they would have belonged to children, but most of those looked much older than the boyfriend's. This Bigfoot had not had any problems with eating humans in the past, but there was nothing that gave a clue as to why it would now be moving further out of its territory and into the nearest human settlement.

Here and there at the base of the pile Crag found bits and pieces of clothing and leather. He poked at the top layers of that with his foot and found that much of the organic material had disintegrated the further he got into the detritus, but there were a few pieces here and there that were obviously very old, like belt buckles and a rusty pipe that looked like it might have once been part or a very old rifle. He even thought he saw a driver's license near the top in one far corner, and rings and necklaces scattered around. Crag dug through and found a few pieces that he thought would be easier to identify and shoved them into his pockets. He was willing to bet that he had here the clues to solve a number of mysterious disappearances over the years.

There were also some markings on the wall of the room, but most of them were in deep corners that weren't touched by the light coming in through the hole near the top. Taking a closer look, he saw primitive stick drawings of things that were obviously supposed to be humans hunting, along with much larger, slightly out-of-proportion humanoids that Crag had to assume were Bigfoots. Crag wasn't an anthropologist, so he had no way of knowing if these cave drawings had been done by indigenous peoples of the region or if a Bigfoot itself had somehow managed to draw these, but they were obviously very old. These creatures had obviously lived in this region for a very long time, much longer than non-indigenous settlers had been here.

"Crag, you still okay down there?" Tennyson called from up top.

"Not eaten by anything yet, kid, although I'd rather not stay down here for much longer and tempt fate."

"Well I found something that might help," Tennyson said. "It's not much, but without going all the way back to Shacksville for a ladder or some rope, it's probably the best we're going to get for now."

"Anything's better than nothing," Crag said. "I

definitely don't think it would be a good idea to sit down here the entire time it would take for you to get down the mountain and then back up. I have a feeling that if you did that, you might not find me sitting here in one piece by the time you returned."

Tennyson dragged a very large, thick tree branch into view. It looked like something that had been knocked down in a storm or – who knew? – ripped down by an inexplicably angry Bigfoot. It seemed strong enough to support Crag's weight, but it would be extremely heavy and awkward for Tennyson to hold while Crag tried to use it to climb up. They didn't have any better options, however, and Crag didn't want to be down here anymore. The longer he stayed, the more he felt like he wouldn't be alone here for long. He kept looking back at that archway leading into a deeper cave system, and every so often he thought he might be able to just barely hear something grunting deep within its tunnels.

Tennyson struggled to maintain his balance and his hold on the branch as Crag awkwardly made his way up it. "You know Crag… for such a scraggly old guy… you're really heavy as shit."

"I may be scraggly, but there's not an ounce of fat on me, Crag said. Anyone else, Tennyson included, probably would have had more trouble climbing up the branch, but Crag hadn't survived as long as he had doing these sorts of investigations by not keeping in shape. He knew plenty of people a quarter of his age that didn't even have a fraction of his physique. Tennyson was straining with his weight, though, and the branch didn't seem like it would hold out for very long.

Somewhere behind him in the cave system, Crag heard a deeper, louder growl that most definitely could not have been his imagination this time.

"Crag," Tennyson said through clenched teeth. "I think… you want… to get up here… faster. Like now."

Crag scrambled the rest of the way up the branch and climbed over the lip of the hole just as Tennyson's strength gave out and the branch fell in on top of the bone pile. The clatter it made felt incredibly loud in the otherwise quiet of the forest.

"No time to rest, kid," Crag said. "I think it would be a very good idea for us to get back down the trail and back to Shacksville ASAP. We can talk more about what we did and didn't find when we're not right at what might be the entrance of a giant hairy monster's home."

"Have to say I agree," Tennyson said. The two of them moved as quickly as they could back to the clearing and then down the trail, the two of them with their guns out the whole way and their ears open for any sign of pursuit. At multiple times during their trip back, Crag thought he heard something following them, but despite how hard they looked, neither of them ever saw the hairy, hulking creature tracking their progress the whole way and noting when they drove off in the direction of the village.

CHAPTER EIGHT

When they got back to town, they both agreed to take some time to reorient themselves, going back to their motel rooms to shower and change into fresh clothes that didn't smell like the festering meat of a possible Bigfoot garbage pile. By the time they finished it was the middle of the afternoon, and they agreed to go to the diner for a late lunch/early supper. By unspoken agreement, though, neither of them discussed the case. Instead they made harmless small talk, mostly about Tennyson's time in the academy and how much it had changed from all the way back in Crag's day. Tennyson even found himself actually enjoying the older man's company, and it was nice to just talk to him in a friendly manner that had nothing to do with murdered college kids or mysterious furry monsters living at the edge of civilization. Eventually, though, they couldn't avoid talking about the case any longer, and Tennyson pulled from his pocket a number of things he'd grabbed from in the hole. He'd mentioned on their way down from the mountain that he had them, but this was the first time Tennyson got a chance to see any of them.

"So what exactly are we looking at here?" Tennyson asked. Crag was careful not to let anyone else in the diner see what he had, but in a far corner Tennyson realized that Doc Aarons was finishing up a hamburger and watching them intently. Crag saw where he was looking and motioned for the doctor to come on over before he could explain any of the items he'd found.

"Is it really a good idea to bring her into this anymore than she already is?" Tennyson asked. "Some of this stuff may provide information we shouldn't exactly be sharing with the general public."

"If there's one thing I've learned investigating

cases like this in my many, many years with the agency, it's that you can't ignore the locals or any extra information they may have," Crag said. "She's already shown herself to be helpful in her own sort of way. If we stay friendly with her, she can continue that way."

"Hey there, boys," she said quietly as she approached their table. Tennyson couldn't help but notice that the waitress and the cook, the only other two people in the diner, saw the three of them meeting and kept themselves as far away as possible. For such a small town, the people around here sure knew how to mind their own business. "Did you have any luck searching for our friend today?"

"I think we did," Crag said. "And if you don't mind, we could use your help going over some of the things we found along the way."

"Wouldn't mind at all, but I suggest we do it somewhere a little more private than here. Back at the clinic again? I've still got plenty of booze to pass around if you need any."

Although it was still a while before sunset, the sun was getting lower toward the trees as they made their way back to Doc Aaron's clinic. Once inside, they spread out all the evidence and files on the doctor's desk, and Crag, despite Tennyson's protests to the contrary, shared all the evidence they had from the file on the death of Jessica LaCroix and her boyfriend, and then proceeded to tell her in detail of everything they had seen and done while up on the trail. Aarons listened quietly for most of it, not speaking again until Crag was finished. She picked up one of the moldering driver's licenses Crag had fished out of the bone pile and studied the name on it.

"I remember hearing about this person," she said as she tapped it. "He went missing just a couple of days before I moved here. I didn't really understand what went on in this town at that time, but it didn't take me long to figure it out from the few tidbits I was able to pry out of locals."

"And I bet that if I compare some of these other pieces to case files for other people reported missing in this area, we'll come up with some more matches," Crag said. "There would probably be even more if we were able to get a full forensic team up here to go through that whole pile."

"Then why don't we?" Tennyson asked. "We

have to have more than enough evidence to get other agents involved in this, right?"

"You'd think so, kid, but unfortunately that's not the way these cases tend to work for me," Crag said. "I've got enough dirt on people in the upper levels that they let me investigate whatever I want, but I don't have enough to get them to invest too many resources in me, especially since so much of this isn't really considered part of our agency's jurisdiction."

"You still haven't told me which agency you're with," Doc Aarons said.

"No, we haven't," Crag said, then went back to talking to Tennyson as though she'd never spoken. "Our people may have a level of training that other agencies don't, but the higher-ups don't think these kind of woo-woo cryptid cases are a good use of our time. If I push for too much, they'll try to shut us down. Trust me on that one. It's happened to me before, and it wasn't easy to get back on it all again."

"You know what's strange, though?" Doc Aarons said. "I'm looking at this stuff you found in there, and I'm realizing how rare it is for people to actually go disappearing around here, considering there are actually hikers and nature lovers that pass through here on a regular basis. It's actually rare for things to get bad enough to attract the sort of attention that you guys bring."

"But why the sudden escalation now?" Tennyson asked. "If these Bigfoots or Bigfeet or whatever you want to call them have been up in these mountains all this time, why are they suddenly becoming so much more savage?"

"They've always been savage," Doc Aarons said. "But they were also deep enough into the forest and mountains that we could pretend most of the time that we didn't realize what was actually out there. In the last few months, though, more people have been disappearing around here than normal. Not just the tourists, either, but the townsfolk, the ones who know better than to mess with anything out there in the wild. Something has changed, but I'll be damned if I could tell you what that something is."

"Something has to have changed recently," Crag said. "You can't think of anything at all that it might be?"

"This is Shacksville," Doc said. "*Nothing* ever

changes around here."

"Has anyone or anything possibly been invading their territory?" Tennyson asked. "Maybe someone trying to do some kind of real estate development or build a road where there maybe shouldn't be one?"

"No one wants real estate around here, and why would anyone want to build a road that doesn't go anywhere? There really is nothing worth having around here except for solitude," she said.

"There's got to be something we're not seeing," Crag said quietly to himself. "Probably something simple that we're not even thinking to consider."

"You two want some whiskey to go with your deep thinking?" Doc Aarons asked. She stood up from her seat, and at first Tennyson thought she was going to the drawer in her desk again. Instead she went into the bathroom, and Tennyson heard her open and then close the medicine cabinet. She came back out with another bottle. "Actually, it looks like I drank all the bathroom whiskey already. Going to have to go with the bathroom tequila instead."

"Is there any place in this building where you don't have a bottle of booze hidden?" Tennyson asked.

"The exam room," Doc Aarons said. "I may be a lush, but I've still got to be professional, right?"

"I've got to say I'm curious," Crag said. "How is it that someone like you came to be a practicing doctor way out in the middle of nowhere like this?"

"What, it's not obvious?" Doc Aarons said as she shook the bottle for emphasis. "I like my drink. Turns out I like my alcohol more than I like practicing medicine in a larger city. But I'm not irresponsible. I know that practicing somewhere else with me being the way I am could get someone hurt or killed. So I found a place where they didn't have anything at all. Here in Shacksville, even a drunk doctor is still better than no doctor at all. If they really don't want to use me, they can do what they all did before and drive somewhere else."

"Do you even make enough money to continue to stay in business?" Tennyson asked.

"I'm not going to get into my background, but let's just say I don't need money. These days I'm much more concerned with just keeping away from the rest of the world. Although I wouldn't say it doesn't get a little lonely around here."

For a moment, Tennyson thought she might have been making a pass at him, which he would have carefully and thoughtfully skirted around. Then he realized that as she was saying it she was staring directly at Crag. While the doctor was older than Tennyson by about twenty years, she had to be twenty or thirty years younger than Crag. The age difference might have seemed weird, but given that they were discussing strategies to hunt down a Bigfoot, "weird" had taken on a completely different meaning than usual for him. Whatever the doctor's intention, Tennyson decided it was simply none of his business.

"I'm sure it does," Crag said, his tone of voice neither confirming or denying his thoughts on the implications of her words.

"So we still haven't decided how we're going to approach this going forward," Tennyson said. "And it's getting pretty late. We need to figure out what our plan is for tomorrow."

"It can't be that late, can it?" Doc Aarons asked. Tennyson responded by showing her the time on his cell phone. They'd been going over all the information and evidence for many hours now, and although there were no windows in this particular room, Tennyson was pretty sure it had to be dark out by now.

"Doc, if you're still willing to help us along on all this, we can be back in the morning," Crag said as he stood up from the chair he'd been in.

"I'm definitely in," Aarons said. "I may have gotten used to living in a town plagued by a fucking Bigfoot, but that doesn't mean I won't take any opportunity to do something about it."

"Great," Tennyson said through a yawn. He and Crag started toward the front door, and Doc Aarons opened it for them so they could go out into the night. "Crag, think we can head back to the diner before we go back to the motel? I'd rather have something in my system other than all the doc's alcohol before we call it a night."

"Sure," Crag said. "I'm betting we can still…"

Something roared at them from outside. They all turned to look across the street. From between the same set of buildings it had come from the night before, they saw a rampaging Bigfoot charging right at them, its hands held out to them with sharpened claws and its jaw opened in a scream of saliva and foam.

For some reason, Tennyson doubted that all it wanted to do to them was say hi.

CHAPTER NINE

Doc Aarons slammed the door shut and bolted it, then immediately backed away in the direction of her office. The Bigfoot hit the door at full speed, but it wasn't enough to send the door completely flying. At best, though, it would only last for one or two more hits.

The doctor ran into her office and the two agents followed, again shutting the door behind them. This one, however, didn't seem to have any kind of lock on it.

"Will one of you two get the fuck over here and help me with this?" Doc Aarons yelled. She was leaning against her huge wooden desk and trying to shove it in the direction of the door but not having much luck. Tennyson ran over to join her and found that, even with the two of them, the thing was so heavy that they had difficulty making it budge. It would definitely block the door long enough to give them some time, but only if they could push it the remaining few feet before the Bigfoot realized which door they were behind and pounded it down. "I don't know if we'll be able to do this," Tennyson said.

"Oh for fuck's sake, both of you get out of the way," Crag said. He shoved Tennyson but was a bit gentler with Doc Aarons, clearing both of them for him to take their place. Tennyson was about to state that there was no way such an old man could move that gigantic desk all by himself, except seconds later Crag was pushing it across the floor so easily that he might as well have been pushing a baby's stroller. He got it flush against the door just in time for something to ram into the door hard from the other side, shaking the wood and visibly cracking it. "Now if both of you are finished screwing around," Crag said, "how about we all get the hell out of here before that thing gets in here and beats us all to death with our own severed limbs?"

And for all the heaviness of the desk and the apparent sturdiness of the door, it did indeed look like the creature on the other side was going to get through sooner rather than later. Tennyson looked around the room, but there weren't exactly a lot of places in here where they could either hide or escape. "Please tell me there's some kind of back door around here that we can get out of?"

"No door, but there's a window in the bathroom that might be just big enough for us to squeeze through," Doc Aarons said. She led the way into the cramped bathroom and shut the door behind them, although this time there was nothing they could use to block the door if the creature managed to get this far. The window in question was definitely not going to be something comfortable to crawl through, but if they could get it open far enough it would still work. The only problem that Tennyson could see was that the window frame seemed to be painted shut. It wasn't going to be easy for them to pull it open. He was ready to start trying it, but before he could, Doc Aarons picked up the lid off the toilet tank and threw it through the glass instead.

"Was that really necessary?" Tennyson asked her.

"Busting the window? Maybe not," she said. She reached into the toilet tank and pulled out a bottle of vodka. "But I needed to get this anyway, so I figured why not?"

"Is this really the best time for more booze?" Tennyson asked.

"Just trust me," Doc Aarons said. "This one's not for drinking."

Tennyson decided they really didn't have the time to ask and started clearing away the shards of glass in the window so they could get through with minimum lacerations. Out in the office he could hear the door splintering and breaking, along with the enraged grunts of something strong and extremely pissed-off. Once it was through that outer door, it would have no problem at all getting through the flimsy door to the bathroom. Once he was sure they wouldn't be cut to shreds, he gestured for Doc Aarons to go through first, then Crag. The two of them shimmied through the small opening while Tennyson kept his gun ready and aimed at the door. There was a tremendous crash from the office that could only have been the desk being shoved or flung with a great deal of force. It would probably only be a matter of seconds before the Bigfoot came through this second door ready to tear him apart.

The instant he saw that Crag was through, he crawled out himself, but as he was coming out the other side, he suddenly had a bad feeling. It was only as he was spilling out onto the ground behind the clinic that he realized all the stomping and roaring from Doc Aarons's office had suddenly stopped. In his mind he tried to calculate how quickly a Bigfoot would have to move to get back through the rooms and then around the building to them, but if he had finished the thought, any calculation he would have come up with would have ended up being too slow. Right as he was standing back up, the Bigfoot came around the side of the building, and Tennyson finally got more than just the fleeting glimpse he'd already had of what it looked like. In many ways, it was exactly what he would have always thought a Bigfoot would look like. Its fur was matted and dirty and covered in leaves and mud, and the teeth in its mouth looked like they could bite his forearm in two with one chomp. And the huge, ill-proportioned thing was running right for them.

"Tennyson, out of the way!" Doc Aarons screamed from behind him, and although he had no idea what she was about to do, he jumped aside with absolutely no hesitation. Something whizzed through the air right where his head had been and smashed into the monster, sending glass shards flying everywhere. Tennyson didn't need her to tell him that it had been the bottle of vodka, and he had an idea of what was about to happen next.

The Bigfoot, enraged and confused at the glass bomb that had just hit it, charged blindly at them. Tennyson was out of the way and Aarons was far enough back, leaving Crag to be the central target of its anger. Crag tried to stumble away, but the creature lashed out with a long kick that hit the older agent hard at the ball of his ankle and sent him sprawling. The Bigfoot appeared about to pounce on him, but its attention on Crag left the doctor with enough of an opening to pull a lighter out of one of her pockets and flick the wheel. The flame caught, and she tossed the lighter into the creature's fur in the dead center of its chest, right where the vodka bottle had exploded.

Tennyson was actually disappointed that the creature didn't go up in a sudden roar of flames, but the actual effect was more than enough for the moment. Whether because the alcohol wasn't strong enough or because the mud caked all over the creature kept the alcohol from soaking too far into the fur, the flame that spread over the Bigfoot moved slowly and stayed concentrated on a small area. Small blaze or not, though, it was enough to cause the Sasquatch to scream in fear and pain before loping off back around the building. Tennyson followed it just far enough to see it head back the direction it came, slamming its chest with its enormous paws in an effort to put the fire out.

And the night was once again quiet as though the Bigfoot had never even been there.

CHAPTER TEN

Although they probably would have been safe staying exactly where they were that moment, none of them felt comfortable staying exactly where a huge rampaging monster had last seen them. They ran a few buildings down to the back of the diner and stopped there by the dumpster behind the building. The business probably should have still been open, but the owners seemed to have shut it early for the evening, possibly in response to the screaming creature wandering around openly in the town's streets. Tennyson couldn't blame them, and he certainly wasn't going to call the Better Business Bureau on them for closing their doors outside of posted business hours.

Neither Tennyson nor Doc Aarons had come out of the attack worse for wear, but Crag had limped terribly all the way to their new hiding spot. Tennyson suspected Crag was the kind of man who could and would hide his injuries whenever he was able, so him showing his limp like this made the younger agent think the damage might be bad indeed. It took some wrangling for him and the doctor to get Crag to sit down long enough for them to look at it, but when he finally did, Crag looked seriously relieved to no longer be standing on it.

"It's nothing, really," Crag said.

Tennyson pulled up Crag's pants leg and hissed at the bruised, swollen mess that was the older agent's ankle. "There's no way you're going to be able to walk on this."

"I've walked on a lot worse injuries than this," Crag said, pushing the pant leg back down. "That doesn't mean it's not going to hurt like a son of a bitch."

Doc Aarons snorted. "Bet the other injury wasn't caused by Bigfoot, though."

"A Mongolian Death Worm, actually," Crag said.

Aarons paused. "I'd say you have to be joking, but you don't look like the kind who is even capable of it."

"You might be surprised," Crag said with a pained smile. "After you've seen all the things I've seen, you learn to take whatever humor you can get and in any form."

"Doc, maybe you should be doing less incredulous staring at him and instead be looking at this?" Tennyson asked. "Is it broken?"

Doc Aarons took a closer look at it and poked it carefully and gingerly. Although Crag was in noticeable pain as she prodded at it, the older agent didn't make any noise or movement during her examination.

"I don't think it's broken," she said after a while, "although I won't be able to tell for certain without an x-ray. Seems more like it's just sprained and severely bruised. I'd avoid walking on it, if I were you."

"You're not me, and that's not exactly something I can avoid right now," Crag said. "Doc, that rampage we just saw. Is that something the local Bigfoot has ever done before? Just come crashing into a building in Shacksville in the middle of the night with no visible provocation?"

"Never," Aarons said. "It's never even come into town as far as I know until last night. So blatantly attacking someone right in town and trying to get into an actual building? It's completely unheard of. No one around here has ever seen anything like it."

"Whatever is going on with it, the situation is escalating," Tennyson said. "If we don't put a stop to it, then the people of the town, as few of them as there are, will all be in danger."

"They could be in danger right now," Doc said. "That thing could have decided that it would be better off going after a few easy targets. It could be breaking into one of the other buildings as we speak."

"I don't think so, at least not yet," Crag said. "I think charring its fur spooked it enough to make it head back to some place it thinks is safe, but who knows for how long. We have to find it and take care of it before that happens."

"If you two are going to try running off after it, then you're on your own," Doc Aarons said. "I'm going to find myself another shotgun and then keep an eye on things here in town."

"Is that really the best option?" Tennyson asked. "We could probably use your help going after it."

"What do you think I am, an idiot? I may tend to be drunker than a skunk, but I'm not suicidal. If I try going up the mountain after it in the dark, I would definitely be the one out of the three of us not coming back down. No thank you, I think I'll let the professionals from the shady government agency do that instead."

"Our agency really isn't that shady," Tennyson said.

"Oh, it isn't? Then tell me again, because I seem to have forgotten: exactly which agency do you work for again?"

"You'll find out if we ever get around to showing you our badges," Crag said.

"Which will be when?" Aarons asked.

"Sometime when we're not worried about a Bigfoot coming back down out of the mountains and killing us all," Crag replied.

"I suppose that's fair," she said grudgingly.

Crag gingerly got to his feet and motioned for

Tennyson to come with him. "We need to get moving. If we're going to go where we think that thing's home might be, we've got a long walk in the dark, and we'll need a few supplies before we can go."

"And if we're going up the mountain," Tennyson said to him, "then we'll need to get you a cane or at least a walking stick. And don't be all macho about it like you won't need it. Both of us are going to need to be at our best condition when we get to that bone pit, and you know you won't be if your leg is screaming holy murder at you."

"I might be able to get my walking stick from the ruins of my office, assuming that wasn't one of the things our Bigfoot decided to obliterate for no apparent reason," Aarons said. "Probably can't help you with the rope, though."

"We'll find some way to make do," Crag said. "Doc, get anything you can that you think will help us and meet us over in the parking lot of the motel. Kid, let's go make sure we're loaded up for a fight. Something tells me this is going to be a very long night."

CHAPTER ELEVEN

The longest part of the night, it turned out, was simply getting back up the mountain trail with the equipment they needed. Crag's walking stick, on loan from the doctor, and the pair of flashlights they took with them were easy enough. It was the ladder they had to bring with them that caused problems. With no rope to be found anywhere (at least not from anyone who was willing to open their doors to strangers in the middle of the night right after a ravenous beast had run around on fire in the middle of Main Street), they'd been forced to "borrow" a ladder that had been leaning against the side of someone's house so they could clean gutters.

Of course, getting back up the mountain while one of them was nursing an injured leg and they were both carrying a large metal ladder was difficult, and no matter how good of condition they both would have been in under other circumstances, they were both winded and tired by the time they reached the clearing with the lone boot and the felled tree. Under better circumstances they could have taken a moment to rest, but neither of them was stupid enough to let their guard down when they were in the domain of a large rampaging monster that they had recently pissed off royally. Still, they at least set the ladder down in the clearing and took a minute to take stock of themselves before they continued.

"Are you really sure you're up to this?" Tennyson asked Crag. The Crag had proven so far to be the toughest old man Tennyson had ever met in his life, but he still couldn't help but be concerned for his condition.

"Whether or not I'm up for it is kind of a moot point, isn't it?" Crag said. "We're here now, and we're probably working against a clock. Any time you think maybe we should rest, just remember that the Bigfoot could have tried to charge into any of those other homes down in Shacksville that wasn't quite as prepared for him as the doc was. I certainly am not willing to have some young family's blood on my hands because I got a little winded and sore. Are you?"

Tennyson certainly could not argue with that.

It wasn't hard to find the general spot where Crag had first wandered into the woods and then found himself tumbling into a pile of bones. But when they looked where they thought it might have been, all they could find was the regular forest floor.

"Right about here," Crag said. "I think I recognize that rock formation over there. I saw it right before the ground gave out under me and I fell into the bone pit."

Tennyson swept the beam of his flashlight over the ground around their feet, but there wasn't any hole to see, or even anything that looked like it could be covering up such a hole. "Are you sure? It's not like that creature could have just covered up a giant cave in the ground full of bones."

"Are you sure about that?" Crag asked as he started to poke the ground in front of him with his walking stick. Tennyson just let him. He had no idea what the older agent thought he was looking for, but he was beginning to trust the Crag's instincts. If someone had told him two days earlier that he would trust his life to a man who believed in Bigfoot and went halfway across the country to chase one, Tennyson would have told that person they were full of shit. After a few pokes, Crag hit a spot where the grass seemed to give far more than it should under the pressure. Bending down was difficult with his bad ankle, but he crouched with a minimum of pained grunts and then took a handful of the grass and brush. He yanked upward and found that the "ground" came up quite easily; it actually seemed to be some kind of primitive woven mesh with leaves and bits of bushes stuck into it to create a surprisingly effective camouflage.

"No way," Tennyson said. "There's no way that thing's smart enough to make something like that."

"After you work enough cases like this, you'll learn better than to say that kind of thing," Crag said. "Just because something isn't human doesn't mean it's mindless."

Although the camo net was crude, it was surprisingly effective at mimicking the regular forest floor, especially in the darkness. As Crag pulled it up, he could see that it was more than large enough to cover up the hole he'd fallen in earlier in the day, and Tennyson helped him pull the surprisingly heavy camouflage away from the entrance to the cave system. In the nighttime darkness, they were unable to see the pile of bones that they both knew was below them. Tennyson shone his flashlight down there but there was no sign of anything new beyond what they had seen earlier in the day.

"Now are we really sure that this is the way in to where this creature lives?" Tennyson asked. "Judging from all the bones, this could just be its version of a trash pile or compost heap."

"There was definitely something beyond that archway down there when we were here this morning," Crag said. "I doubt this is the main entrance to this thing's home, but at the very least it's some kind of back door."

They went back and grabbed the ladder from where they'd left it in the clearing, then proceeded to extend it and then lower it into the hole. It was barely long enough, and considering it was balanced on a stack of bones they were lucky that it managed to stay stable long enough for both of them to get down into the bottom of the hole. Crag went first, moving gingerly on his injured (and likely hurting and throbbing like a son-of-a-bitch after walking all the way back up the trail) leg, while Tennyson covered him with his gun. Then Tennyson followed him down, and despite Crag's best efforts to keep the ladder steady, the bone pile shifted beneath it and sent Tennyson tumbling the last few feet into the hole. It didn't really hurt him, but he could see immediately that the bone pile had shifted enough that the top of the ladder would no longer reach the lip of the hole. They could probably get back up this way, but not without spending a great deal of time stacking the bones back up into something stable they could rest the ladder on.

And to make matters worse, Tennyson found as he got up from his fall that in the process, he'd smashed his flashlight. They weren't the sturdiest of things to begin with, having been whatever Doc Aarons could get on sale around here, and there was no way Tennyson would be able to repair it as they went into the cave.

"We're down to only one flashlight," Tennyson

said to Crag. "I'm not exactly liking how this is starting to turn out."

"If you're losing your nerve, kid, I'm not going to blame you," Crag said. "Not everyone is cut out for hunting cryptids and things. But if you're going to bail out on me, you better do it now. I don't want to be in there next to you and have you completely lose it at the worst possible moment."

"Have I seriously given you any reason so far for you to think I would do that?" Tennyson asked, trying hard not to sound offended.

"Not at all. Not even close. I'm just giving you that one last chance to stay here."

"Fuck that," Tennyson said. "I'm your partner. I might not have wanted to be at first, and I may have fought you at several points along the way but I do not ever turn my back on someone who's relying on me, got it?"

"I definitely do, kid, and I'm glad to hear it," Crag said with a smile.

And with that he led the way through the archway and deep into what they believed was the lair of the Bigfoot.

CHAPTER TWELVE

The bad news started right away within the first two minutes when the second flashlight died. To the best of their knowledge, nothing had damaged it like the first. It just seemed that Doc Aarons hadn't bothered to keep a very close eye on how much battery power they had left. Neither of the agents said anything to each other as the light flickered and faded before dying. They didn't need to. There simply seemed to be an unspoken agreement between them that the lack of light wasn't going to be enough to send them scrambling back where they had come, no matter how dangerous it became.

But as much as the deeper darkness toyed with Tennyson's mind, it still wasn't the thing that freaked him out the most. That came when he started hearing growling coming from deeper in the cave.

Tennyson wildly pointed his gun around in the dark, but the cave's acoustics made it impossible for him to be certain where the sound was coming from.

"Crag," he whispered, "if you can hear me, I'm pretty sure we're not alone."

"No shit," the old man's voice whispered back. "With that kind of detective work, no wonder you were the star of the academy."

"You're lucky I can't see you right now, or I might shoot you in the foot. Your good one."

The grunt came again, and this time it was definitely closer. "Pretty sure that whatever is in here with us, it isn't human and it isn't something like a bear," Tennyson said.

"No, it's not," Crag said carefully. "But I think it's even worse than that. Listen again."

They both went completely silent until they heard another grunt. This one seemed further away than before, but also seemed like an entirely different pitch, like something similar but smaller than the thing that had made the first noise. As if to get rid of any doubt, there was another, deeper grunt than the first one, and it seemed the closest of them all.

"There's more than one," Tennyson said, now taking much more care than earlier to keep his voice around a whisper.

"At least three," Crag whispered back. "And one of them is getting closer."

"Crag, we should get out of here," Tennyson said. "We should be calling in some help."

"It would take too long for anyone to get here," Crag said. "If we leave now, these things could descend on the town at any time and do to the entire place what a single one of them did to the clinic. More people would die. And while I have to say I have respect for her, I don't exactly trust Doc Aarons to shoot straight, if you know what I mean."

"So this is it, then, huh?" Tennyson asked. "Our chance to be the big damned heroes?"

"You know you've been waiting for it, kid," Crag said. "This is your chance to show me if all that talk about how great you were at the academy was bullshit or not."

Tennyson pulled out his gun and cocked it. "It wasn't bullshit."

Crag did the same with his own gun. "Then let's find us some Bigfoot."

Despite the bravado of their proclamations, neither of them could run headlong after their prey in the dark. While neither of them had flashlights, it took Tennyson an embarrassingly long moment to realize he could at least give himself some kind of light using the screen on his phone. That didn't work out for him, though, as when he pulled it from his pocket, he found that it had been cracked and broken at some point during the night's earlier excitement. He called out to Crag to check the same thing, only to find that the other agent must have dropped his phone at some point, most likely when they were fleeing out the window of the clinic. Without any source of illumination at all, they were not going to be at any advantage when they finally came face to face with these things. Despite the near total darkness, though, Tennyson did find that his eyes adjusted a limited amount so at the very least he didn't blunder blindly into any walls.

The tunnels they were in seemed to be mostly natural, but occasionally Tennyson felt the rock walls to find his way and found them smoother than he would expect, like someone or something had carved portions of the stone away a very long time ago. He thought back to what Crag had said earlier about the cave paintings and wondered if some earlier group of people had once used these caves as their home before the Sasquatch creatures had come, or if somehow it was the Bigfoots themselves who had managed to carve parts of these tunnels out. Either possibility left a lot of unanswered questions that Tennyson didn't think they would get a chance to investigate, at least not at this time. That might be a case for a later date, assuming they survived this case first.

Although the two of them made an effort to stay together, Tennyson found it difficult unless they were physically touching at all times. The tunnels expanded and contracted, sometimes bringing the walls close together enough that it made Tennyson a little claustrophobic, and sometimes expanding so far that the two of them wouldn't be able to touch either side if they both touched a wall with one hand and reached out to their partner with the other. Distances were hard to judge, and Tennyson quickly lost track of how far they had come.

"Crag, I really hope you've been keeping track of where we're going," Tennyson said, "because at this point, I think I'm completely lost."

He waited for a moment for an answer, but Crag said nothing.

"Crag? You still there?"

"Hush up, kid," Crag whispered. "Listen. Do you hear it?"

Tennyson stood absolutely still and listened in the dark, but at first all he could hear was the hard pounding of his pulse in his own ears. Then, after several seconds of straining, he did hear something. Something was moving along the cave toward them in a slow, shuffling gait. It actually didn't sound quite as large as Tennyson would have expected it to be, so at first he thought it really did have to be some other kind of animal rather than one of their Bigfoots. The sounds were accompanied by some kind of snuffled moaning, however, and Tennyson couldn't imagine what kind of animal that might be.

It got closer and closer until Tennyson was sure it was nearly on top of them. He had his gun out and ready to fire, but Crag was the old hand here, and for some reason the elder agent wasn't acting like he was ready to attack. Tennyson would have asked him what he thought he was doing, but if Crag had gone completely quiet then Tennyson would too.

Tennyson smelled the stink of rancid fur bearing down on him. The presence in the darkness paused, snuffling lightly like it was smelling the air. Then the noises started to recede in another direction like the creature had found another tunnel nearby that Tennyson hadn't even guessed existed. As the sounds of movement got farther and farther away, the young agent released the breath that, until now, he hadn't even realized he was holding.

"Crag?" Tennyson whispered. "Please tell me you're still there."

"I'm still here," Crag said, but his voice had some distance to it, as though he had wandered further away in the dark while Tennyson wasn't paying attention.

"That was a close one," Tennyson said.

"Was it, though?" Crag asked. "I'm not so sure it was."

"What do you mean?" Tennyson asked.

"I mean I'm starting to wonder if all the creatures we heard down here are equally dangerous.

Just hear me out here, but what if…"

He didn't get a chance to finish his thought. From somewhere behind them something horrid yowled at them, and then the cave was filled with the sound of large, pounding footsteps heading right for them. Tennyson spun and aimed his gun in that direction, but whatever it was whooshed past him. It was brief, but as it ran past, he was pretty certain he caught the slightest scent of singed fur. Tennyson thought he heard a grunt from elsewhere in the tunnel, then the clatter of metal on rock as Crag dropped his gun. Then the pounding, howling demon sounds were receding, and the cave again grew quiet.

"Crag?" Tennyson asked the darkness. "Are you alright? Did that thing hurt you?"

Only silence responded to him.

"Crag? Please tell me you're still there."

But the quiet of the tunnels was all Tennyson needed to hear to realize he was now completely alone in this labyrinth below the earth.

CHAPTER THIRTEEN

Crag had heard the creature coming at them, but he had not been fast enough to do anything about it. He may have gone to great lengths to ensure that he stayed remarkably strong even at his age, but no matter how much he worked out, there was only so much he could do to keep his speed up. And, while he would not admit it to Tennyson, the pain in his ankle was occasionally bad enough to keep him from thinking straight. So when the creature had barreled down the tunnel and run right into him, his reaction time had not quite been enough to keep him from getting the wind knocked out of him and having his gun thrown to deep parts unknown.

He had expected the Bigfoot to rip him apart right then and there, but instead he found himself hoisted up on the creature's shoulder as it continued on with its break-neck pace through the tunnel. Somewhere behind him he thought he heard Tennyson calling out for him, but Crag was too dazed at first to shout back. Soon enough Tennyson's voice disappeared completely, and Crag found himself alone with a rampaging Sasquatch.

Multiple times during their brief journey, the Bigfoot accidentally – or maybe not so accidentally at all – smashed him into either the roof of the cave or the side of the wall. Crag did his best not to make any sound when it did that, instead acting limp and unconscious in its arms. They didn't go very far, although the creature did seem to zig-zag through multiple tunnels like it was trying to get Tennyson to lose its trail. By the time they finally halted, Crag himself doubted that he would be able to find his way back the way they had come without a lot of trial and error.

Judging from the sounds of the echoes as the Bigfoot grunted, they were now in a larger chamber than any that they had been in previously.

Instinctively, Crag realized this was probably the monster's main living area, and it sounded like it was more than large enough to hold more than one of them. Sure enough, as the Bigfoot not-at-all gently dropped Crag to the floor in front of it, Crag could hear the echoes of other guttural, inhuman voices. Just as they had guessed earlier, there seemed to be two more for a total of three. And seconds later, just as Crag had guessed a few minutes ago but hadn't had a chance to pass on to Tennyson, he confirmed another theory.

This wasn't just three random Bigfoots. This was a family: two parents and something that might have been a child.

The three beasts crowded around Crag. The smallest of the creatures reached out and touched Crag's throbbing leg, doing so with a gentleness that he never would have expected from something so inhuman. This close, he was finally able to make out details of the thing's face even in the blackness of the caves. The Bigfoot (although Mediumfoot might have been a better name for this one, given how much smaller it was than the others) had a face that seemed like a cross between that of a human and an orangutan, only a lot hairier than both put together. Although it was the smallest of them, Crag estimated that it would probably be about five and a half feet high when fully erect. Around average for a human, but tiny for these things.

Before the smaller one could touch him, the largest of the Bigfoots snarled and lashed out, cuffing the little one hard upside the head. The small one wailed in pain, and Crag had a flashback to long ago in his childhood, of an abusive father hauling off on his son because he was drunk and belligerent and eager to take out his anger against the world on something that wouldn't fight back. Crag recognized an abused child when he saw it, and the sight, even if the child wasn't human, made his blood boil.

But there was another detail about the largest one that Crag could see now that it was close enough to haul off on the small one. The largest creature, presumably the matriarch or patriarch or whatever kind of leader these things had, had tendrils of foam running from the edge of its mouth. With that, Crag thought he suddenly had a good idea of why the attacks over the past days had been getting worse. The biggest one, the leader, was sick. Maybe it was rabies, or maybe it was some kind of illness that only affected these creatures, but whatever the problem was, Crag suspected it was causing the Bigfoot to lose whatever mind it had. The other large one looked like it might have been crazed, too, but then Crag couldn't exactly say for certain what a non-crazed Bigfoot would even look like.

The smallest of the three backed away from Crag, leaving the leader to hulk over him and drool on his leg. Although Crag had lost his gun somewhere back when the Bigfoot had grabbed him, he always kept a knife strapped to his calf hidden under his pant leg. It was a habit that had gotten him out of many jams in the past, but it wasn't something he thought he could get out in time if he made a sudden move right now. This thing would be able to rip him apart before he was able to get free. The only way he was going to be able to defend himself was if he found a way to distract it first.

Luckily for him, he wasn't the one who had to come up with a distraction. Elsewhere in the tunnels there was a rattle of rocks and muttered cursing, the sure sign that Tennyson wasn't far and was on his way. The middle of the three Bigfoots grunted and went in the direction of the sound, leaving only the large one and the small one in this chamber with Crag. Now all he needed was for the biggest to find something else to focus on for at least a few seconds while Crag pulled for the knife.

As much as Crag would have preferred not to direct the leader's rage at the smallest one, it seemed like the only real option at the moment. While the Biggestfoot was slightly distracted with the departure of its second-in-command, Crag scooped up a loose rock from next to where he was sitting and tossed it over in the direction of the small one. The big one turned and roared at the little one, taking a step toward it in a threatening manner, and Crag took that moment to pull up his pants leg and go for the knife. The creature turned back to him just as he was pulling it from its sheath, but it didn't give any indication that it realized he was now armed. Instead it went back to hunkering over him menacingly, its jaws gnashing together and raining more foaming spittle on Crag's clothes. Crag didn't lunge with the knife yet, instead waiting to see what the monster would do.

What it was going to do, it turned out, was go

for Crag's head like it was about to rip it off his neck so it could start eating the juicy meat inside his body. With a speed that anyone else would have likely been shocked to see in a man his age, Crag thrust the knife up into the creature's hand right as it grabbed for his face. It screamed and pulled back, giving Crag just enough time to scramble to his feet and try running in a random direction.

He didn't get far until he ran into something large and furry. Crag's initial thought was that this was it, that he was finally about to meet his end, before he realized it wasn't the largest of the Bigfoots that he'd run into. It was the smallest, the Mediumfoot, and at this distance, Crag could look right into its eyes and see a level of intelligence and sanity that he hadn't seen in the other two.

While the largest of the creatures continued to scream and flail about somewhere else in the darkness, the Mediumfoot made some kind of unidentifiable gesture, then started to run off into the darkness.

Crag, not being sure that it was a good idea but not having a clue of what else he could do, followed it as fast as his bum leg would let him.

CHAPTER FOURTEEN

Tennyson heard the creatures long before he got anywhere close to them. The acoustics in these tunnels and caves were strange, so he couldn't always be certain whether he was heading toward the grunts and grumbles or away from them, but he did his best to keep a calm and level head each time he had to stop and orient himself to make sure he was facing in their direction. At the very least he didn't hear death screams of anguish coming from Crag as the Bigfoots turned him into dinner, but then again, he wouldn't be surprised if the Crag stayed silent while he was eaten just to spite his killers.

The closer he got to the sounds, though, the

more he found he was muttering and cursing to himself before he caught what he was doing and forced himself to be silent again. While the creatures sure sounded like they were occupied with something, he didn't want to risk giving away his position.

The quality of the echoes changed, and Tennyson got the impression that the tunnel in front of him spread out into a much larger cave. He only barely had time to register this fact and what it might mean for him before something rushed at him from the emptiness right in front of him.

It wasn't quite right to say that the Bigfoot lashed out with a punch. That implied a level of finesse or control that these creatures didn't seem to possess. It was more like the creature swung its entire arm as though it were a long wooden club, and the back of its fist connected solidly with Tennyson's ribcage. He found himself lifting up off the floor and flying backward into the cave wall, causing his vision to flash bright with pain. When he hit the floor his gun flew out of his hands and slid off somewhere on the cave floor.

Tennyson had only a moment to decide whether

he was going to chase after the gun or try to take on the Bigfoots without it. Although his chance of finding the gun in this darkness was slim, he still figured it would give him a better chance than if he tried to fight this hulking monstrosity in a straight up test of strength. He scurried low over the stone floor as something whooshed over his head. The stink of unwashed fur made him think it was probably another punch, but it hadn't come close to him this time. In this situation, apparently being so tall was a disadvantage. A wild swing like that would always be high.

Tennyson groped around in the darkness, hoping he was in the general vicinity of his weapon, and after a few more seconds, he found the barrel. Behind him in the darkness he could hear Crag struggling, although whether it was with the smallest of the three or the medium, he couldn't be sure. All he knew was that if the biggest of the Bigfoots got in one more really good punch on him, he would probably pass out and never again wake up, instead ending up as the latest addition to their pile of bones.

Tennyson properly took the gun by the grip and spun around as fast as he could, aiming it in the general direction in the dark where he thought the Bigfoot had to be. Concentrating on the sounds around him, he thought he heard the creature coming for him slightly to the right of where he was aiming. Without hesitating, he adjusted his aim and fired.

In the brief flash from his gun, Tennyson saw the Bigfoot lunging directly for him and right into the path of the bullet. The flash didn't stay in the air long enough for Tennyson to see if any blood splattered, but the creature gave a hideous, unearthly roar that echoed through the tunnels and very clearly signaled that it was in a great deal of pain. The bullet didn't seem like it had been a killing shot, though, so Tennyson readjusted his weapon to follow the scream and fired again. This time the noise that came from it was more of a whine than a roar, and Tennyson knew that he must have hit something vital. It wasn't until he heard something huge thump to the cave floor, though, that he thought he might have actually turned the tables on the situation. He continued to keep the gun pointed out in front of him, just in case, as he heard the monster gurgle and whine in what seemed to be a death rattle. It seemed likely that Tennyson had managed to shoot it directly in the lungs.

Just to be sure, though, Tennyson moved closer until he could feel the fur of the creature and put a bullet into where he thought the creature's head was. All sound from it stopped, and Tennyson was positive that it was completely dead. There was no way this thing was going to get back up and jump at him for one last scare.

Elsewhere in the darkness, Tennyson could hear the grunting of a struggle, but he couldn't be sure if the noise was coming from Crag or from one of the creatures. Unless Crag had managed to do something while he'd been down here alone to take one of the monsters out, Tennyson was pretty sure there were at least two of them left. His gun had a fifteen-bullet magazine, and so far tonight he'd only used three. He also had another magazine in the pocket of his jacket, so he wasn't terribly worried about running out of bullets just yet. He was more concerned with shooting wildly in the dark and accidentally hitting Crag. He hadn't scored the highest numbers on his marksmanship tests just to accidentally miss and wound his partner right out of the gate on his very first case.

"Crag?" Tennyson asked, his voice in something like a shouted whisper. "Crag, are you there? Can you hear me?"

The main response he heard back was a roar as another Bigfoot, this one apparently larger even than the first one he'd taken down, came running at him from somewhere in the dark. Tennyson raised his weapon to fire again, but this time before he could something leaped out of the shadows and slammed into the monster. Tennyson's first thought was that it had to be Crag, but he doubted that Crag could move with the fury and anger that this thing did. To his surprise, Tennyson suddenly realized that the thing that had come to his rescue was another, albeit smaller, Bigfoot.

"Don't shoot it! That one's on our side!" Crag called out from somewhere in the darkness, not that Tennyson needed his partner to give him that revelation. For whatever reason, the smaller of the two creatures seemed to have no interest in attacking either Crag or Tennyson, instead leasing the full power of its unholy fury on its elder. As the over-sized fists flew at each other, Tennyson realized he could see slightly better in here now than he'd been able to deeper in the network of tunnels. They had to be somewhere close to an entrance if light was filtering through, and morning had to already be coming. It gave him a better view as the two creatures wailed on each other like whirlwinds. Although the one that was apparently on their side had a very significant size disadvantage on the other one, their own personal Bigfoot seemed to be more focused, maybe even more intelligent. The larger one looked like it was getting winded easier. Maybe that was because of the burnt patches up and down the front of its torso, or maybe it had something to do with the thick foam spitting from its lips. Even though the big one might not have survived in a prolonged battle, Tennyson was pretty sure it could prevail if it just got in a few lucky punches. And if that happened, both the agents and their unexpected ally would likely be dead.

Tennyson took a deep breath and raised his gun at the whirling storm of hairy limbs.

"Kid, watch it!" Crag called out to him. "It's too dark for you to get a good shot. If you miss…"

"I won't miss, old man," Tennyson responded, although the words were soft enough that they may have just been intended for himself rather than his partner. Carefully sighting down the barrel, adjusting for the action of the battle, and in the end just letting a little bit of instinct and luck guide him, Tennyson exhaled and then fired.

The top of the enormous Bigfoot's head blew off in an explosion of blood, bone, and brain matter. It let out one last keening howl that almost sounded like a question, then let go completely of its fellow combatant. The smaller one dropped to the stone floor, looked at the larger monster, and gave a sad hoot before scrambling away into the darkness where Tennyson lost all track of it. The remaining Bigfoot, already dead or dying but too large for all of its body to get that message at once, pawed nonsensically at the air in front of its face.

Then it keeled over onto the floor. What few brains were still in its head splattered out the hole in its skull and spilled over the floor. There was a putrid stink that suggested the very last thing the Bigfoot did before all traces of life completely left it was piss and shit itself.

Tennyson, realizing he was still holding the gun up in front of him, slowly lowered it.

Somewhere nearby, Crag grunted as he got to his feet and hobbled over next to Tennyson. He could see the old man fairly clearly now, and it was obvious that the old man was smiling.

"I told you I was the best shot back at the academy," Tennyson said to him. Crag slapped him heartily on the shoulder.

"Yeah, you sure did, kid. Now what do you say we find a way out of this shithole?"

"Breakfast is on me," Tennyson said wearily.

"Hell, screw breakfast," Crag said. "I think I'm finally ready to partake in some of the good doctor's stash of booze."

Tennyson thought that sounded pretty damned good as well.

CHAPTER FIFTEEN

Once again, Agent Bradley Tennyson sat across from the department head in his office as the boss stared at him. This time, however, he'd just finished reading Tennyson's after-action report, and the look he was giving Tennyson was one of pure, unrestricted disbelief and skepticism.

"Tennyson, please tell me you don't actually expect me to believe any of this," the boss man said.

"It's one hundred percent true," Tennyson said. Not that the report Tennyson had turned in contained every single detail of what had gone down in Shacksville. He'd left a few details out, but not anything that would hide the fact that the two agents had legitimately faced down a family of Bigfoots and won. The biggest detail missing was that the Crag, despite his advanced age, had gone to spend an awfully long amount of alone time with Doc Aarons before the two agents had headed back out of the tiny mountain town. Tennyson figured that Crag had earned a little bit of time to enjoy himself after that whole encounter. Who knew? Maybe Crag and Aarons had simply spent that time talking and tending to his swollen leg. But Tennyson really doubted it. It wasn't exactly a thought he wanted to dwell on.

The department head closed the file he'd been reading and then sighed. "You know, I don't really know what else I expected. It's not like I expected you to make Agent Crag change his mind about some of his crazy ideas, but I'd hoped that a different perspective would prove all the things he keeps rambling on about to be wrong."

"You don't believe the things Crag says he investigates, sir?" Tennyson asked.

"I don't know if I'd say I don't believe him. A part of me has always just hoped the old man was going senile, I guess. I suppose it's a little much to hope you're going senile too, huh?"

Tennyson tried to continue looking professional instead of offended. "I'm twenty-one. I really don't think I'm anywhere near the level of being senile yet."

"Yeah, that's what I was afraid of," the boss man said. "I'll bury this file deep where most people won't find it, just like so many other files Agent Crag leaves me. You're dismissed, but I wouldn't head home just yet. Crag wanted to see you down in his lair."

Tennyson had already suspected that and, surprisingly, had looked forward to it. Although he now knew the short-cut down into the Crag's moldy little corner of the cold case archives, Tennyson instead went in the same general direction he had on that first day. It no longer felt so strange or foreboding down here, and he no longer found himself getting lost at all along the twisted path and many hallways. And as he entered the enormous cold-case storage room for only the second time, he already got the strange feeling like he was walking into something that could truly be his home.

The Crag was back at his table with his laptop

in front of him, just as he had been a few days earlier when they'd first met. He had a brand-new storage box in front of him, and he was loading it both with the paper copies of the case file and all the pieces of physical evidence they had gathered over the last couple of days, from the driver's licenses of long-lost Bigfoot victims to evidence bags with samples of Bigfoot hair. If this were considered a more legitimate operation by the rest of the agency, all of that would probably be in a lab somewhere right now getting tested for all manner of things. Instead it was all ready to be packed away and forgotten like so many other boxes of strange evidence on the shelves surrounding them.

"I should let you know that I talked to the doctor earlier," Crag said when he saw Tennyson approaching. "She said she and a couple of other locals went up to the cave. No one wanted to go in very deep, but they said they could find no sign of the Mediumfoot. It looks like it has vanished somewhere deeper into the mountains."

"As long as it doesn't go rabid like the other two, I'm personally okay with letting it go off and do its own thing," Tennyson said.

"I was actually kind of surprised you didn't try to kill it when you had the chance in that cave."

"Not only did it help us," Tennyson said, "but I don't see any reason in destroying it purely because it's some monster out of legend."

"It's a good thing for me to hear that," Crag said. "You may in fact be surprised how often that attitude has kept me alive in the massive number of cryptid hunts I've been on."

"Aren't we at least going to have someone go back to that cave and investigate it further? There have to be more secrets in there worth finding, given what we already saw in the bone pit."

"If at some point I have some free time, I might just do that," Crag said. "There might be more tunnels in that underground network than we thought, and there could be other evidence that Bigfoots exist. But if I were you, I wouldn't hold your breath for the agency to send anyone else out to do a more thorough examination. What you see right here going into this box is going to be pretty much all the official material from this investigation, if our little adventure ever technically gets classified as official to begin with."

"So they're just going to bury the whole incident down here in this maze of dusty shelves?" Tennyson asked.

"Of course they are," Crag said. "It's not like they haven't done it before." Crag gestured around at the maze of shelves and boxes and filing cabinets and strange bric-a-brac. "Every single box, file folder, and book in this area is some creature that defies easy characterization. Many that I personally investigated, but many more from before my time that are just waiting for someone to pull it down and open a strange and forgotten case back up."

Tennyson looked around at the shelves around him with a new appreciation. "But they can't all be as bad as what we just encountered, right?"

"Bad? Kid, that was good. I've had cases that went way further south than this one. Barely anyone died for once, and if you don't mind, that's more than enough for me to count it in the plus column. And it certainly was healthier for my mental state than some of them get. When I've got a whole lot of extra time on my hands some time, remind me to tell you about my fourth encounter with the Mothman."

"Fourth?" Tennyson asked. A few days earlier

he would have been completely disbelieving, and he still supposed that, with Crag's sense of humor, he could still very well be pulling his leg. Now though, after what he'd seen, he was less inclined to think the Crag might be joking. "You've actually had four separate encounters with the Mothman?"

"That's right," the Crag said. "And if you're willing to stick around with me long enough, you might even be here for the fifth time."

"Are you really that certain that there will be a fifth time?"

"You wouldn't have to ask that if you knew the Mothman. That crazy motherfucker doesn't leave well enough alone."

It seemed highly likely that the old man was bullshitting him, but then again, after what he'd now seen, maybe the Crag was one hundred percent telling the truth. Tennyson stared long and hard at all the old moldering boxes with a new appreciation and – dare he even say it? – excitement. "A whole bunch of old secrets down here," Tennyson said. "All of them weird, and none of them with anyone taking them seriously enough to investigate them?"

"That's my life, kid," Crag said. "So the

question now is if you want it to be your life, too."

"You're acting like I have a choice in the matter. It was made very clear early on that I didn't," Tennyson said.

"You may not have had at the beginning, but you most definitely do now. I know you made an agreement with the boss man upstairs. He wasn't going to force you to stay my partner after more than one case. And I'm not going to hold you to anything, either. I don't want someone by my side who doesn't want to be there. Although I'm definitely hoping you stay. I do think I might have finally found the correct fit for me in a partner."

It was the first time since he'd talked to their boss on the phone that night at the motel that Tennyson had stopped to consider he might still have any kind of choice in the matter. At the start of this all, he never would have thought he'd want anything more than to get away from the Crag and his moldy basement room as fast as possible.

But now all he desperately wanted to do was pull one of those boxes down and rummage through it until he found their next case. Who knew what kind of secrets and mysteries might be waiting for them that even the Crag himself had not had time to find and investigate yet? "Is every case going to be like this one?" Tennyson asked.

"No," Crag said. "Most definitely not. This one was easy compared to some of the stuff we're probably going to face."

"Excellent," Tennyson said, already moving to take down a random box and look through it. He set it on the table next to the Crag's laptop and removed the lid with a flourish. "Then let's get started."

THE END